THE ORPHAN'S CHRISTMAS HYMN

RACHEL DOWNING

CORNERSTONETALES.COM

A FATEFUL CHRISTMAS EVE

The kitchen of the Winters' cottage glowed with warmth, bathed in the soft golden light of the crackling fireplace. Clara sat at the worn wooden table, her legs swinging beneath her chair, unable to reach the floor. The aroma of fresh-baked bread wafted through the air, its comforting scent wrapping around her like a warm blanket.

"Silent night, holy night," Clara's mother began, her melodious voice filling the cosy space. Clara joined in, her clear, sweet tones blending seamlessly with her mother's.

"All is calm, all is bright," they sang together, their voices rising and falling in perfect harmony.

Clara's father leaned against the kitchen counter, a contented smile playing on his lips as he listened. The firelight danced across his face, highlighting the laughter lines around his eyes.

"Round yon virgin, mother and child," Clara continued, her young voice growing more confident with each verse. Her mother's alto provided a rich foundation for Clara's soprano, the two voices intertwining like strands of silk.

As they sang, Clara's father began to recount a Christmas

story from his childhood. His deep, soothing voice wove between the notes of the hymn, creating a tapestry of sound and memory.

"Holy infant, so tender and mild," mother and daughter sang, their eyes meeting in a moment of shared joy.

Clara's father paused his tale, watching his wife and daughter with undisguised pride. "Listen to that," he said softly, shaking his head in wonder. "Our little nightingale, she is. You've certainly inherited your mother's talent, Clara."

Clara beamed at the praise, her cheeks flushing with pleasure. Her mother reached out and squeezed her hand, a warm smile lighting up her face.

"Sleep in heavenly peace," they finished together, their voices fading to a whisper. "Sleep in heavenly peace."

As the last notes of "Silent Night" faded away, Clara's attention was drawn to the window. The world outside had transformed into a winter wonderland. Soft, fluffy snowflakes drifted lazily from the sky, blanketing the ground in a pristine white carpet. The bare branches of the trees were adorned with a delicate frosting, glistening in the pale winter light.

Clara pressed her nose against the cold glass, her breath fogging up the pane. The familiar landscape of their town had been transformed into something magical, like a scene from one of her father's bedtime stories. Even the old oak tree in their yard, usually so imposing, looked soft and inviting under its snowy mantle.

"Clara, love, come away from the window," her mother called, bustling about the kitchen. "We need to get ready for the Christmas Eve service."

Clara reluctantly tore herself away from the enchanting view. She could hear her father outside, his muffled voice carrying through the walls as he prepared the horses for their journey to the church.

"Jane!" her father called from outside. "We'd best be off soon. The horses are ready!"

Clara's mother paused in her hurried preparations, a worried frown creasing her brow. She peered out the window, her eyes scanning the thickening snowfall.

"George," she called back in concern, "are you sure we should go? The weather's turning worse."

Clara watched as her father appeared in the doorway, snow dusting his broad shoulders and clinging to his beard. His cheeks were ruddy from the cold, but his eyes twinkled with reassurance.

"Don't fret, my dear," he said, crossing the room to place a comforting hand on his wife's shoulder. "The church isn't far, and I've seen worse weather than this. We'll be back home before the heavy snow sets in, I promise."

Clara nestled between her mother and the window as they got in the carriage, the warmth of their bodies fought back the chill seeping through the wooden frame. Looking out the window, she could see the snowflakes dance in the lantern light. Her small fingers traced patterns on the glass, leaving ephemeral designs that quickly faded.

"We'll need to stock up on flour," her mother mused, her voice soft and melodic even when discussing mundane matters. "And perhaps some extra candles for the long winter nights."

Clara's father nodded, his strong hands steady on the reins. "Aye, and we mustn't forget a treat or two for our little songbird here," he said, winking at Clara.

A smile bloomed on Clara's face, and she began to hum "God Rest Ye Merry, Gentlemen" under her breath. The familiar tune filled the small space of the carriage, mingling with the gentle creaking of the wheels and the muffled clip-clop of the horses' hooves.

Her mother joined in, harmonising with Clara's melody. Their voices twined together, rising and falling like the snowy hills around them. Joy surged through Clara, her heart swelling with love for her parents and the simple pleasure of singing together.

As they rounded a bend in the road, the church spire came into view, its cross barely visible through the swirling snow. Clara's excitement bubbled over, and she clapped her mitten covered hands together.

"Look, Papa! We're almost there!"

Her father chuckled, the sound rich and warm. "Indeed we are, my love. And not a moment too soon – it seems the snow is picking up."

Clara hardly noticed the thickening snowfall, too caught up in the magic of the evening. The carriage windows were now almost completely frosted over, but she could still make out the warm glow of lanterns from nearby houses. It was as if the whole world had been transformed into a glittering wonderland, just for Christmas Eve.

As they drew closer to the church, the faint strains of an organ could be heard, playing the opening notes of "O Come, All Ye Faithful." Clara's heart leapt with anticipation, and she began to sing along softly, her parents joining in without hesitation.

The carriage was filled with their harmonious voices, a cocoon of warmth and love amidst the winter night. Clara felt safe and cherished, surrounded by her parents and the joyous sounds of Christmas. In that moment, everything was perfect.

Clara's heart leapt into her throat as the horses' frightened whinnies pierced the air. The carriage lurched violently, throwing her against her mother's side. Jane's arm instinctively wrapped around her daughter, holding her close.

"George!" Jane cried out, her voice tight with fear.

Clara felt the carriage tilt precariously, the world outside becoming a dizzying blur of white. The comforting sounds of their hymn was cut off by the terrifying screech of metal against ice and the thunderous pounding of hooves.

"Hold on!" George's voice was strained as he fought to control the panicking horses.

Clara squeezed her eyes shut, burying her face in her mother's coat. She could feel her mother's rapid heartbeat, matching the frantic rhythm of her own.

The carriage slid sideways, and Clara heard her father grunt with effort as he tried to steer them back on course. For a moment, it seemed as though they might regain control. Then came a sickening lurch as the carriage wheels left the road entirely.

There was a deafening crack as they smashed through the wooden barrier at the road's edge. Splinters flew past the windows, and Clara felt herself being thrown forward. Her mother's arms tightened around her, shielding her from the impact.

The world spun wildly, snow and sky blurring together in a dizzying whirl. Clara heard her mother's prayer, barely audible above the chaos: "Lord, protect us."

Then came the jolting impact as the carriage struck something solid. The last thing Clara registered was her father calling out their names, his voice filled with a fear she had never heard before.

THE WRECKAGE

Clara's eyes fluttered open, her vision blurry and unfocused. The world around her was a haze of white, snowflakes drifting lazily through the air. She blinked, trying to make sense of her surroundings. The interior of the carriage was now a twisted maze of splintered wood and torn fabric.

A sharp pain lanced through her head as she tried to move. Clara winced, her small hand reaching up to touch her temple. Her fingers came away sticky with blood.

The silence pressed in on her, broken only by the soft whisper of falling snow. Where was the clip-clop of hooves, the creak of wheels? Where were Mama's soothing hymns and Papa's hearty laughter?

"Mama?" Clara's voice came out as a hoarse whisper. She cleared her throat and tried again, louder this time. "Papa?"

No answer came. Panic began to rise in Clara, threatening to choke her. Clara struggled to sit up, pushing aside a tangle of blankets and shattered wood. Her dress caught on a jagged splinter, tearing as she pulled herself free.

The cold hit her like a physical blow. Clara gasped, her

THE ORPHAN'S CHRISTMAS HYMN

breath forming little clouds in the frigid air. She wrapped her arms around herself, shivering violently as she looked around.

The carriage lay on its side, half-buried in a snowdrift. One of the doors hung askew, offering a glimpse of the winter landscape beyond. Clara crawled towards it, her movements clumsy and uncoordinated.

"Mama! Papa!" She called out again, her voice stronger now but tinged with desperation. The words echoed across the empty field, bouncing back to her, mockingly empty.

Clara pushed herself through the broken door, tumbling out onto the snow-covered ground. The cold bit through her thin stockings, numbing her legs almost instantly. She struggled to her feet, stumbling as she turned in a circle, searching for any sign of her parents.

"Please," she whimpered, tears beginning to freeze on her cheeks. "Where are you?"

Clara's small feet sank into the deep snow as she stumbled forward, her eyes darting frantically around the carriage. The wind howled, carrying her desperate cries into the night.

She rounded the wreckage of the carriage, her breath ragged and uneven. Two dark shapes lay motionless in the snow, partially obscured by the gently falling flakes. Clara's world narrowed to those still forms, her feet carrying her forward without conscious thought.

"Mama? Papa?" Her voice trembled as she dropped to her knees beside them. The cold bit into her skin, but she barely noticed. With shaking hands, she brushed the snow from her father's face. His eyes were closed, his skin pale and waxy in the moonlight.

"Papa, wake up," Clara pleaded, her small hands gripping his coat. She shook him gently, then with increasing urgency. "Please, Papa. We need to go home."

When he didn't respond, she turned to her mother. Her golden hair was spread out on the snow like a halo, her face peaceful as if in sleep. Clara's fingers traced her mother's cheek, recoiling at the unnatural coldness of her skin.

"Mama," she whispered, her voice breaking. "Mama, please. I'm scared."

The silence stretched on, broken only by the whisper of falling snow and Clara's ragged breathing. Slowly, terribly, the truth began to seep into her young mind. Her parents weren't sleeping. They weren't going to wake up, no matter how much she begged or cried.

A keening wail rose from deep within Clara's chest, a sound of pure anguish that shattered the stillness of the night. It started low, a mournful cry that grew in volume and pitch until it became a haunting, screeching sound.

Clara's wails echoed across the snowy field, a haunting melody of grief that pierced the night. Her small body shook with each sob, her hands clutching desperately at her parents' cold forms. She barely registered the sound of approaching voices, the crunch of boots in snow growing louder.

"Over here!" a gruff voice called out. "I've found them!"

Familiar faces from the church appeared through the swirling snow, their expressions of horror and sorrow. Clara's tear-streaked face turned towards them, her blue eyes wide with desperation.

"Please," she whimpered, her voice hoarse from crying. "Help them."

A weathered farmer knelt beside her, his calloused hand gentle on her shoulder. "Come now, little one," he said gently. "We need to get you warm."

Clara shook her head violently, clinging tighter to her mother's dress. "No! I can't leave them. They'll be cold."

The farmer exchanged a pained glance with the others. A woman Clara recognised from church stepped forward, her arms outstretched. "Clara, sweetheart," she said softly. "Your parents... they're with God now. We need to take care of you."

Clara's mind reeled, unable to fully comprehend the finality of what had happened. She allowed herself to be lifted, her body limp with exhaustion and grief. As they carried her away, her eyes remained fixed on the still forms of her parents, growing smaller in the distance.

The farmer's cart creaked as they settled Clara into it, wrapping her in thick blankets. The wood was rough beneath her, so different from the soft cushions of their carriage. Clara's tears had slowed, replaced by a numbing emptiness that seemed to swallow her whole.

As the cart began to move, jostling over the uneven ground, Clara's lips parted. A soft, wavering tune drifted out, barely audible above the wind. "Silent night, holy night," she sang, her voice trembling. "All is calm, all is bright."

The familiar melody wrapped around her like a comforting embrace, a tenuous link to the warmth and love she'd known just hours before. Clara closed her eyes, losing herself in the hymn as the cart carried her towards an uncertain future.

OLD BELONGINGS FOR A NEW LIFE

Clara huddled in the back of the cart, her small frame shivering despite the thick blankets wrapped around her. The farmer's gentle voice barely registered as he explained their determined destination. St Mary's Orphanage, but first they would go to her home.

As they approached her home, Clara's heart clenched. The familiar sight of the cottage, once warm and inviting, now seemed cold and empty. She stumbled out of the cart, her legs weak beneath her.

"We need to gather some of your things, little one," the farmer said, his weathered hand steadying her. "Can you be brave for me?"

Clara nodded, her throat too tight for words. She thought of her parents, of their love and courage. "I'll be brave," she whispered, more to herself than to the farmer. "For Mama and Papa."

Inside, the cottage felt eerily quiet. Clara moved through the rooms like a ghost, gathering a few clothes and precious items. Her fingers brushed against the leather-bound hymnal her father had given her last Christmas. She clutched it tight, a tangible piece of the life she was leaving behind.

As she packed her meagre belongings into a small bag, Clara's eyes fell on a family portrait. Her parents' smiling faces looked back at her, frozen in a moment of happiness. She traced their features with a trembling finger, trying to memorize every detail.

"I'll make you proud," she promised softly, slipping the photo into her bag.

The farmer waited patiently by the door, his kind eyes filled with sympathy. "Ready, child? Let's get your face washed before we leave."

Clara took one last look around the cottage, her home for all of her seven years. She nodded, unable to speak.

As they climbed back into the cart, Clara held her bag close, the hymnal a comforting weight against her chest. The horses' hooves clopped against the frozen ground, each step taking her further from everything she'd known.

THE CART'S wheels crunched to a halt, and Clara's heart sank as she gazed up at the looming edifice of St Mary's Orphanage. The grim brick structure stretched before her, its windows like empty eyes staring down at her small form. Clara shivered, clutching her leather-bound hymnal to her chest as if it could shield her from the cold.

The farmer helped her down from the cart. Clara's feet touched the frozen ground, and she felt the last threads of her old life slipping away. She stood there, rooted to the spot, unable to take a step towards the forbidding building.

The creak of the heavy wooden door drew Clara's attention. A tall, austere woman emerged, her steel-grey hair pulled back in a severe bun. Her eyes, the same steely shade as her hair, fixed on Clara with a piercing gaze that seemed to strip away any lingering warmth from the child's world.

"You must be Clara Winters," the woman said, her voice as cold and brittle as the winter air. "I am Mrs Blackthorn, headmistress of St Mary's." She turned to the farmer. "We received a message that she would be coming imminently. Such an awful accident."

Clara nodded mutely, her fingers tightening around her hymnal. Mrs Blackthorn's eyes flicked to the book, a flicker of something – disapproval, perhaps – crossing her face before it settled back into its impassive mask.

"Bring your belongings inside. Follow me." Mrs Blackthorn said.

Without waiting for a response, she turned on her heel and strode back into the orphanage. Clara hesitated, her feet refusing to move. The farmer placed a comforting hand on her shoulder.

"Go on, little one," he said softly. "It'll be alright."

Clara took a deep breath, summoning every ounce of courage she possessed. With trembling steps, she followed Mrs Blackthorn into St. Mary's.

A COLD EMBRACE

Clara followed Mrs Blackthorn through the dimly lit hallways of St. Mary's, her small feet struggling to keep up with the headmistress's brisk pace. The walls, painted a dull grey, seemed to close in around her as they walked. Clara clutched her hymnal tighter, seeking comfort in its familiar weight.

"Pay attention, child," Mrs Blackthorn's sharp voice cut through Clara's thoughts. "I'll not repeat myself. Breakfast is at six sharp. Anyone late goes without. Beds are to be made with hospital corners before morning prayers. No exceptions."

Clara nodded silently, her eyes wide as she tried to absorb the torrent of information. Mrs Blackthorn's words blurred together, a harsh symphony of "don'ts" and "mustn'ts" that made Clara's head spin.

"No running in the halls. No raised voices. No frivolous activities." Mrs Blackthorn's gaze swept over Clara's hymnal disapprovingly. "And absolutely no singing outside of approved church services."

Clara's heart sank at those words. Singing had always been her solace, her connection to happier times. She opened her mouth to protest but thought better of it, shrinking under Mrs Blackthorn's stern glare.

They reached a heavy wooden door, and Mrs Blackthorn pushed it open without ceremony. "This is where you'll sleep," she announced, ushering Clara into a large, draughty room.

Clara stepped inside, her eyes adjusting to the gloom. Row upon row of iron bedsteads stretched before her, each topped with a thin, lumpy mattress. The room smelled of dust and despair, a far cry from the cosy warmth of her childhood bedroom.

As Clara stood there, overwhelmed by the stark reality of her new home, she became aware of whispers and furtive glances. Other children, some her age and some older, peered at her from behind bedposts and around corners. Their faces were a mix of curiosity and wariness, sizing up the newest addition to their ranks.

"That's the new girl," one voice hissed.

"Wonder what her story is," another replied.

Clara's small hands trembled as she smoothed down the coarse blanket on her new bed. The iron frame creaked under her weight as she perched on the edge, her feet barely touching the cold wooden floor.

Mrs Blackthorn had taken her leave, telling Clara to get changed and into bed, as it was already far past the normal bed time.

As she changed into her nightgown, Clara felt dozens of curious eyes upon her. She kept her head down, focusing on the task at hand, willing herself not to cry in front of these strangers. But as she climbed into bed, the finality of her situation crashed over her like a wave.

The thin mattress offered little comfort, so different from her plush bed at home. Clara curled into herself, pulling the scratchy blanket up to her chin. In the darkness, with no one watching, she finally let the tears fall. They streamed silently down her cheeks, soaking into the pillow beneath her head.

Clara's chest ached with grief, her breath coming in shuddering gasps as she tried to muffle her sobs. She missed her parents so fiercely it felt like a physical pain. The memory of their voices, their warmth, seemed to mock her in this cold, unfamiliar place.

As she lay there, drowning in sorrow, Clara's hand brushed against something solid beneath her pillow. Her hymnal. She'd tucked it there as soon as she had been assigned the bed, a small act of defiance against Mrs Blackthorn's rules. Now, she pulled it out, running her fingers over the worn leather cover.

Without thinking, Clara began to sing. Her voice was barely above a whisper at first, trembling and tear-stained. But as the familiar words of "Silent Night" filled her mouth, she felt a spark of joy. Her voice grew stronger, sweet and clear in the stillness of the dormitory.

"Silent night, holy night,
All is calm, all is bright..."

The hymn wrapped around her like a comforting embrace, and for a moment, Clara could almost imagine her parents' voices joining hers in harmony.

Clara's soft voice carried through the dormitory, a gentle melody in the darkness. The other children, who had been whispering and fidgeting, fell silent. Some lifted their heads from their pillows, straining to hear the beautiful sound.

As Clara sang, she felt the weight in her chest lighten just a little. The familiar hymn brought a small measure of comfort, reminding her of happier times. She closed her eyes, losing herself in the music.

Suddenly, a harsh voice shattered the peaceful moment. "Whoever is singing, better stop right now! It's bed time!"

Clara's eyes flew open, her heart racing. Mrs Blackthorn's angry tone echoed through the dormitory, causing several children to gasp and quickly burrow under their blankets. Clara snapped her mouth shut, clutching her hymnal tightly.

For a moment, she held her breath, terrified that Mrs Blackthorn would burst into the room and discover her. But the headmistress's footsteps faded away, leaving behind a tense silence.

Clara's momentary peace vanished, replaced by a crushing wave of loneliness and fear. She curled into herself, burying her face in her pillow to muffle her sobs. Tears flowed freely now, soaking the thin fabric.

What would happen to her now? How could she possibly survive in this cold, unwelcoming place without her parents? The thought of facing each day alone, without their love and guidance, seemed unbearable.

As Clara cried, her body shook with the force of her grief. She wanted nothing more than to feel her mother's comforting embrace or hear her father's reassuring voice. But they were gone, and she was left behind in this strange, frightening world.

Exhaustion finally overtook her, and Clara's sobs gradually quieted. Her eyes, swollen from crying, began to droop. As she drifted off into an uneasy sleep, her last thoughts were of her parents and the life she had lost.

A DEFIANT SONG

Clara's knees ached as she scrubbed the worn floorboards, her fingers raw from the harsh lye soap and icy water. The common room of St Mary's Orphanage loomed around her, a cavernous space of stone and shadows. Frost etched delicate patterns on the barred windows, mocking the children with glimpses of a world beyond their reach.

Two months had passed since Clara arrived, yet the chill of the place still seeped into her bones. She'd grown accustomed to the endless chores, the meagre meals, the strict routines that governed every waking moment. But the coldness – both physical and emotional – remained a constant companion.

As she worked, Clara's lips moved almost of their own accord, a quiet melody rising from deep within her:

"Hark! The herald angels sing,

Glory to the newborn King..."

Her voice, though barely above a whisper, carried a warmth that seemed at odds with their bleak surroundings. It floated through the room, wrapping around the huddled groups of children like a comforting blanket.

Clara didn't dare sing loudly, not after Mrs Blackthorn's

stern warnings, but she couldn't stop the music entirely. It was a part of her, as essential as breathing. So she hummed and sang under her breath, finding solace in the familiar hymns.

As she moved her rag in rhythmic circles, Clara noticed a few of the younger children inching closer. Their eyes, usually dull with resignation, now held a spark of interest. One little girl, no more than five, began to sway slightly to the gentle melody.

Clara offered them a small smile, her voice growing just a fraction louder:

"Peace on earth and mercy mild,

God and sinners reconciled..."

For a moment, the oppressive atmosphere of St Mary's seemed to lift. The cold stone walls faded into the background, and Clara could almost imagine herself back in her parents' cosy kitchen, their voices joining hers in joyful harmony.

Clara's soft singing was abruptly cut short as the common room door swung open with a bang. Mrs Blackthorn swept in, her tall frame casting a long shadow across the floor. Her eyes narrowed as they fixed on Clara, who froze mid-scrub.

"Miss Winters," Mrs Blackthorn's voice cracked like a whip. "So you're the one responsible for all this... caterwauling."

Clara's cheeks burned as she lowered her gaze to the floor. The other children scattered, leaving her alone before Mrs Blackthorn's imposing figure.

"Look at me when I'm speaking to you, girl," Mrs Blackthorn snapped.

Clara raised her eyes, meeting the headmistress's icy stare. Mrs Blackthorn's lips were pressed into a thin, disapproving line.

"This orphanage is not a music hall, Miss Winters. Your singing is frivolous and distracts from the importance of discipline and work. We are here to mold you into productive members of society, not indulge in idle fancies."

Each word felt like a blow, chipping away at the small kernel of joy Clara had managed to nurture. She blinked rapidly, willing away the tears that threatened to spill.

"Yes, Mrs Blackthorn," Clara mumbled, her voice barely audible.

"I won't hear another note from you, is that clear? Now, finish your chores in silence."

With a final withering glance, Mrs Blackthorn turned on her heel and strode out of the room. The door slammed behind her, the sound echoing in the sudden, oppressive quiet.

Clara bent her head over her scrub brush once more, her movements mechanical. The room felt colder now, as if Mrs Blackthorn's presence had sucked away what little warmth remained. But deep within her, a tiny flame of defiance flickered. Music was part of who she was, a connection to her parents and her faith. She couldn't – wouldn't – let that be taken away.

As the evening wore on and the children settled into their nightly routines, Clara found herself in the scullery, up to her elbows in soapy water as she tackled a mountain of dishes. With Mrs Blackthorn safely ensconced in her office, Clara allowed herself to hum softly, the melody only just louder than the splash of water.

REVEREND THORNTON

Reverend William Thornton stepped out of his carriage, his breath misting in the crisp February air. He tugged his woollen coat tighter around his shoulders and gazed up at the imposing facade of St Mary's Orphanage. The building loomed before him, all gray stone and barred windows, a stark contrast to the cheery vicarage he'd left behind.

William squared his shoulders and approached the heavy wooden door. He'd heard whispers about the strict regime at St Mary's, but he believed in giving everyone the benefit of the doubt. With a silent prayer for wisdom and compassion, he raised the brass knocker and let it fall.

The door creaked open, revealing a stern-faced woman with grey hair pulled back into a tight bun. "You're the new Parish Vicar, Reverend Thornton, I presume," she said, her voice as crisp as the morning air.

"Indeed, Mrs Blackthorn," William replied, offering a warm smile. "It's a pleasure to make your acquaintance."

Mrs Blackthorn's expression didn't soften, but she stepped aside to let him enter. "Welcome to St Mary's. I trust you'll find everything in order."

THE ORPHAN'S CHRISTMAS HYMN

As they moved through the corridors, William's keen eyes took in every detail. The floors were spotless, the walls bare save for a few stern biblical quotes. Children scurried past, eyes downcast, their footsteps eerily quiet on the worn floorboards.

"We run a tight ship here, Reverend," Mrs Blackthorn explained, her voice echoing in the austere hallways. "Structure and discipline are paramount in molding these children into productive members of society."

William nodded, his smile never wavering. "Of course, Mrs. Blackthorn. Structure is important. But so too is nurturing the spirit, wouldn't you agree?"

Before Mrs Blackthorn could respond, a faint sound caught William's ear. It was barely audible, a whisper of melody floating on the air. His heart lifted at the sound, so incongruous with the somber atmosphere of the orphanage.

William followed the ethereal sound, his footsteps light on the worn floorboards. Mrs Blackthorn's voice faded into the background as he rounded a corner, drawn by the haunting melody. The singing grew clearer, and William's heart swelled with each note.

He found himself outside the laundry room, the door slightly ajar. Peering inside, he saw a young girl with auburn hair, her back to him as she worked over a steaming washtub. Her voice, pure and clear, filled the room with the strains of 'O Holy Night'.

William stood transfixed, barely breathing for fear of interrupting the beautiful performance. The girl's voice soared on the high notes, infusing each word with raw emotion that belied her young age. Her small frame swayed gently as she sang, her hands never ceasing their work even as her spirit seemed to transcend the dreary laundry room.

As the final notes faded away, William felt a lump in his throat and moisture in his eyes. He had heard professional choirs in grand cathedrals, but never had he been so moved by a single voice. The purity of the girl's tone, the depth of feeling in her interpretation – it spoke of a rare and precious gift.

William cleared his throat softly, drawing Mrs Blackthorn's attention. Her eyes narrowed as she realised where he'd wandered off to.

"Mrs Blackthorn," he began, his voice gentle but firm, "I believe I've just heard something truly extraordinary. That young girl's voice... it's a gift from God Himself."

Mrs Blackthorn's lips pressed into a thin line. "Reverend, I assure you—"

"No, please," William interrupted, his eyes alight with enthusiasm. "You must understand. In all my years, I've never heard such pure talent. It would be a disservice to keep it hidden away."

He took a step closer, his voice lowering conspiratorially. "I propose we have her join the church choir for the Easter service. Her voice could inspire the entire congregation."

Mrs Blackthorn's face tightened, her disapproval evident in every line. "Reverend Thornton," she said, her voice clipped, "while I appreciate your... enthusiasm, I must object. We run a structured environment here. Allowing one child special privileges would disrupt our entire system."

William watched as she straightened her already impeccable posture. "Moreover," she continued, "it would be a distraction from the girl's duties and the discipline we strive to instil in all our charges."

"But surely," William pressed, his tone gentle but insistent, "nurturing such a talent would be beneficial? It could open doors for her future, provide hope—"

"Hope?" Mrs Blackthorn's eyebrow arched. "Reverend, we deal in practicalities here. These children need structure and skills for the real world, not fanciful dreams."

William took a deep breath, his eyes meeting Mrs Blackthorn's steely gaze. He could see the resistance in her rigid posture, but he refused to back down. This wasn't just about music; it was about nurturing a soul.

"Mrs Blackthorn," he began, "I understand your concerns. But music... music has the power to heal, to uplift, to bring light into the darkest corners of our lives." He gestured towards the laundry room where the girl's voice had filled the air moments ago. "That child's voice is a rare and precious gift. In a place like this, where hope can be scarce, shouldn't we cherish such a blessing?"

William watched as Mrs Blackthorn's expression flickered, a hint of uncertainty breaking through her stern facade. He pressed on, his voice gentle but firm. "Think of the joy her singing could bring to the other children, to the entire congregation. It could be a beacon of hope, a reminder that even in the bleakest circumstances, beauty can flourish."

Mrs Blackthorn's lips thinned. For a long moment, silence stretched between them, broken only by the distant sounds of children and the hum of daily orphanage life.

Finally, Mrs Blackthorn let out a long, controlled breath. "Very well, Reverend," she said, her voice clipped. "The girl may join your choir for the Easter service." She raised a warning finger, her eyes hard. "But let me be clear: this will not interfere with her chores or the discipline we maintain here. She is to fulfil all her duties without complaint or special treatment. Is that understood?"

William nodded, relief and joy flooding through him. "Of course, Mrs Blackthorn. You have my word."

THE CHURCH CHOIR

Clara's hands were raw and red from scrubbing, her fingers pruned from the soapy water. She hummed softly to herself, finding solace in the familiar melody of 'O Holy Night'. The laundry room's dampness clung to her skin, but the music warmed her from within.

Footsteps echoed in the corridor outside, growing louder. Clara's shoulders tensed, expecting Mrs Blackthorn's sharp rebuke. Instead, a gentle knock preceded the creak of the door.

A tall man with kind eyes and salt-and-pepper hair stepped into the room. His clerical collar marked him as a man of the cloth. Clara's curiosity piqued, but she kept her head bowed, unsure of how to act.

"Hello there, young lady," the man's voice was warm and rich. "I'm Reverend William Thornton, the new Parish Vicar."

Clara looked up, meeting his gaze. His eyes crinkled as he smiled, and she felt a flicker of something she hadn't experienced in her entire time at St Mary's – hope.

"I couldn't help but overhear your beautiful singing," Reverend Thornton continued. "Tell me, would you like to join our church choir?"

Clara's heart leapt. She blinked, certain she had misheard. "The... the choir, sir?"

He nodded, his smile growing wider. "Indeed. We could use a voice like yours for our Easter service."

A warmth blossomed in Clara's chest, spreading through her body. She felt lighter, as if a great weight had been lifted from her shoulders. A shy smile tugged at the corners of her mouth, growing until it lit up her entire face.

"I'd love to, Reverend," she whispered, her voice thick with emotion. "Thank you."

CLARA'S HEART raced as she approached St Paul's Church for her first choir rehearsal. The stone building loomed before her. She hesitated at the heavy wooden doors, her fingers tracing the intricate carvings.

As she stepped inside, shafts of coloured light streamed through the stained-glass windows, painting the nave in a kaleidoscope of hues. The beauty of it all made her chest ache with a bittersweet longing for her parents and the Christmases they'd shared.

"Welcome, Clara," Reverend Thornton's warm voice startled her from her reverie. He stood beside a tall, thin man with wire-rimmed spectacles. "This is Mr Hawthorne, our choir director."

Mr Hawthorne nodded with a warm smile. "Reverend Thornton tells me you have quite the voice, young lady. Let's hear what you can do."

Clara swallowed hard, suddenly aware of the other choir members watching her. But as the first notes of "Christ the Lord is Risen Today" rang out, she felt her anxiety melt away. Her voice, tentative at first, grew stronger with each verse.

"Wonderful, Clara!" Reverend Thornton beamed. "You're a natural."

Mr Hawthorne adjusted his glasses, his eyes sparkling with excitement. "Indeed. Now, let's try it again, this time with everyone."

As Clara's voice blended with the others, she felt a warmth spreading through her chest. For the first time since losing her parents, she felt truly at peace. The music wrapped around her like a comforting embrace, lifting her spirit higher with each note.

THE EASTER SERVICE

Clara's hands trembled as she smoothed down her choir robe. The simple white garment felt foreign against her skin, a stark contrast to the patched and faded dresses she'd grown accustomed to at St Mary's. She took a deep breath, inhaling the aroma of incense that permeated the church.

The pews were packed, a sea of faces turned expectantly towards the choir. Clara's eyes darted nervously around, searching for a familiar face. She caught sight of Mrs Blackthorn, sitting stiffly in the back row.

As the first notes of "Jesus Christ is Risen Today" filled the air, a sudden calm washed over Clara. She opened her mouth, and her clear, pure voice rose above the others. The congregation seemed to hold its collective breath, captivated by the angelic sound.

Clara lost herself in the music, her eyes closed as she poured her heart into every word. She thought of her parents, imagining them smiling down at her from Heaven. For the first time since their passing, the memory brought more comfort than pain.

When she opened her eyes, she noticed several people in the

congregation dabbing at their eyes with handkerchiefs. Even Mrs Blackthorn's stern expression had softened somewhat.

As the final notes faded away, Clara's gaze met Reverend Thornton's. He stood at the pulpit, his face beaming with pride and joy. In that moment, Clara felt a surge of gratitude for the kind-hearted vicar who had given her this opportunity.

The reverend gave her a small nod, a gesture full of warmth and understanding. Clara returned it with a shy smile, feeling a newfound sense of belonging wash over her.

EDWARD THORNTON

Clara's fingers moved deftly as she wrung out a damp cloth, her eyes squinting against the bright sunlight streaming through the orphanage windows. The summer morning had brought a rare warmth to St Mary's, softening the usual gloom that hung over the place like a shroud.

She hummed softly to herself as she wiped down the worn wooden tables in the dining hall, her auburn hair catching the light and seeming to glow. At thirteen, Clara had grown taller, her limbs longer and more graceful, but her eyes still held that same spark of hope they always had.

As she worked, her mind wandered to the upcoming Sunday service. Reverend Thornton had requested her presence in the choir once again, and the thought made her heart soar. She could already hear the swelling notes of the hymns, feel the comfort of being surrounded by other voices raised in harmony.

Of course, Mrs Blackthorn had put up her usual resistance. Clara had overheard the headmistress's sharp words through her office door just yesterday.

"The girl has responsibilities here, Reverend. She can't go gallivanting off to sing every time you snap your fingers."

But as always, Reverend Thornton's gentle persistence had won out. His calm voice had floated through the door, soothing Mrs Blackthorn's ruffled feathers.

"My dear Mrs Blackthorn, surely we can spare Clara for a few hours. Her voice is a gift, and it brings such joy to our congregation."

Clara smiled to herself, grateful for the reverend's unwavering support. She didn't know how she would have survived these past years without the solace of music, without those precious hours spent in the church, her voice rising to the rafters.

As she moved on to the next table, Clara began to sing softly, her clear voice filling the empty dining hall. For a moment, the dreary orphanage faded away, and she was transported to a place of peace and beauty, where the music never ended.

EDWARD THORNTON SHIFTED UNCOMFORTABLY in his best suit as he followed his father through the iron gates of St Mary's Orphanage. At fifteen, he'd finally been deemed old enough to accompany Reverend Thornton on one of his pastoral visits. He found himself tugging at his collar, trying to loosen it just a bit.

"Remember, son," his father said, placing a hand on Edward's shoulder, "these children have faced great hardship. A kind word can mean the world to them."

Edward nodded, swallowing hard. He'd seen the orphans at church, of course, but this was different. This was their home, such as it was.

As they approached the main entrance, a stern-faced woman Edward recognised as Mrs Blackthorn emerged to greet them. Her eyes seemed to bore right through Edward.

"Reverend Thornton," she said, her voice as crisp as her starched collar. "And this must be young Edward."

Edward's father smiled warmly. "Indeed, Mrs Blackthorn. Edward's been eager to join me on these visits. I thought it high time he learned the importance of community outreach."

As the adults fell into conversation, Edward found his attention wandering. A faint melody drifted on the air, drawing him towards the courtyard. He recognised the tune – it was one of the hymns they'd sung in church just last Sunday.

Rounding the corner, Edward's breath caught in his throat. There, in the midst of the dusty courtyard, stood a girl about his age. Her auburn hair gleamed in the weak sunlight as she sang, her voice clear and pure as a mountain stream. It was the girl from the choir, the one whose solo had brought tears to half the congregation's eyes.

Edward stood transfixed, afraid to move lest he break the spell of her song. He'd never heard anything quite like it outside of church. Here, in this grim place, her voice seemed to transform the very air around her, filling it with a warmth and hope that defied the orphanage's grey walls.

The girl's song trailed off, her eyes widening in surprise as she noticed him. He felt a flush creep up his neck, realising he'd been caught staring. But there was something about her that made him want to stay, to hear her sing again.

"Hello," he said, summoning up his courage. "I'm Edward. Edward Thornton." He flashed what he hoped was a winning smile. "That was beautiful, by the way. Your singing, I mean."

The girl ducked her head, a pretty blush colouring her cheeks. "Thank you," she murmured, peeking up at him through her lashes. "I'm Clara."

Their eyes met, and Edward felt a jolt of... something. Recognition, perhaps, or a spark of kinship. He cleared his throat. "I've seen you in the choir. Your voice is really something special."

Clara's smile brightened, and Edward found himself grinning back. "Do you sing too?" she asked.

"A bit," Edward admitted. "But what I really want to do is conduct. I'm hoping to become a choirmaster someday."

Clara's face lit up with genuine interest. "Really? That's wonderful!" She took a step closer, her earlier shyness forgotten. "What's your favourite piece to conduct?"

Edward launched into an enthusiastic description of a Bach cantata he'd been studying. Clara listened intently, nodding along even though some of the terms were unfamiliar to her.

"I don't know many composers by name," she confessed. "But I love learning new hymns. There's one we sang last week that I can't get out of my head..."

As Clara hummed a few bars, Edward's eyes widened in recognition. "Oh, I know that one! It's from..."

They fell into an easy conversation about music, trading favourite melodies and discussing the emotions different songs stirred in them. Edward found himself captivated by Clara's passion and the way her eyes sparkled when she talked about singing.

Edward found himself looking forward to the visits to St Mary's with an eagerness that surprised him. Each time his father announced they'd be going, Edward's heart would skip a beat, knowing he'd have a chance to see Clara again.

On one such visit, Edward managed to slip away while his father was deep in conversation with Mrs Blackthorn. He found Clara in the courtyard, her hands raw from scrubbing laundry, but her eyes bright as ever.

"I brought you something," Edward said, glancing around to make sure they weren't being watched. He pulled a folded sheet of music from his jacket pocket.

Clara's face lit up as she carefully unfolded the paper. "Oh, Edward! It's beautiful," she breathed, her fingers tracing the notes. "But I can't keep this here. Mrs Blackthorn would..."

Edward nodded, understanding. "We could practice it together now?" he suggested. "Just quietly."

They huddled close, heads bent over the music. Edward hummed the melody softly while Clara picked up the harmony. Their voices blended seamlessly, and for a moment, the dreary orphanage faded away.

As weeks passed, Edward found more excuses to visit St Mary's. He'd offer to help with odd jobs or deliver messages for his father. Each time, he'd seek out Clara, even if only for a few precious minutes.

They shared whispered conversations about their dreams – Edward's aspirations to conduct great choirs, Clara's hope to one day teach music to children. Edward found himself captivated by Clara's resilience, the way she found beauty in even the simplest melodies.

One afternoon, Edward arrived to find Clara looking particularly downcast. "What's wrong?" he asked, concern etching his features.

Clara sighed, her shoulders slumping. "Mrs Blackthorn caught me singing while mopping floors. She's forbidden me from humming even to myself now."

Edward's heart ached for her. Without thinking, he reached out and squeezed her hand. "We'll find a way," he promised. "Music is too important to give up."

As he said the words, Edward realised how true they were. Not just the music, but Clara herself had become important to him in a way he couldn't quite explain. Their friendship was a bright spot in both their lives, a shared language of melodies and dreams that transcended the walls of St Mary's.

SILENCED

Clara's heart soared every time Edward visited St Mary's. His presence brought a warmth to the cold, austere halls of the orphanage that she hadn't felt since losing her parents. As the months passed, their friendship blossomed like a delicate flower pushing through cracks in concrete.

They'd steal moments together whenever possible, Edward sneaking sheet music to Clara or teaching her new melodies in hushed whispers. Clara's eyes would light up, her voice a soft, melodious whisper as she learned each new song.

But Mrs Blackthorn's sharp eyes missed nothing. She noted the spring in Clara's step, the brightness in her eyes that hadn't been there before. Where once there had been a compliant, somber child, now stood a girl who hummed under her breath as she worked, whose smile came more readily.

Mrs Blackthorn's lips thinned to a hard line. This would not do.

"Clara!" she barked one afternoon, catching the girl absent-mindedly dusting the same shelf for the third time. "I see you have energy to spare. The scullery needs a thorough scrubbing. See to it immediately."

Clara's shoulders slumped, but she nodded. "Yes, Mrs Blackthorn."

As days wore on, Mrs Blackthorn's rebukes grew more frequent, her assignments more gruelling. Clara was forced to scrub floors long after the other children had gone to bed, mending twice her usual share of clothes, and relegated to the stuffiest, most unpleasant chores in the orphanage.

"Idle hands lead to mischief," Mrs Blackthorn would say, her steely gaze boring into Clara. "We must keep you occupied, mustn't we?"

Clara's newfound joy dimmed under the onslaught of extra work and harsh words. Her hands grew raw from scrubbing, her back ached from hours of bending over mending.

∼

Arms laden with freshly laundered sheets, Clara's muscles ached as she trudged down the dimly lit hallway. The setting sun cast long shadows through the orphanage's grimy windows, marking the end of another exhausting day. As she neared Mrs Blackthorn's office, hushed voices drifted through the partially open door.

"That Clara girl is becoming a nuisance," Mrs Blackthorn's sharp tone cut through the air. "All this singing nonsense has given her ideas above her station."

Clara froze, her heart pounding. She inched closer to the door, straining to hear more.

"And that Thornton boy," Mrs Blackthorn continued, her voice dripping with disdain. "Filling her head with dreams and music. It'll only lead to heartache, mark my words."

The bundle of sheets slipped from Clara's trembling hands, hitting the floor with a soft thud. Tears pricked at her eyes, a mix of hurt and anger welling up inside her. Before she could stop herself, she burst through the door.

"Why do you hate me so much?" Clara cried, her voice cracking. "What have I done wrong?"

Mrs Blackthorn's head snapped up, her eyes narrowing. "Clara Winters! How dare you eavesdrop and barge in here uninvited?"

"You're always so cruel to me," Clara pressed on, her words tumbling out in a rush. "You give me more chores than anyone else, you never let me sing unless it's for church. Why?"

Mrs Blackthorn rose from her chair, her tall frame looming over Clara. "You foolish girl," she said, her voice cold and flat. "You think you're special because of your voice? Because the Reverend's son pays you attention?"

She leaned in close, her breath hot on Clara's face. "Let me tell you something, child. That boy will forget all about you the moment he leaves for university. And your singing? It's a frivolous distraction that will bring you nothing but disappointment. The only reason I allow you to have anything to do with that church and those Thorntons is because you're not worth the trouble it would take to convince them to just leave us alone!"

Clara stumbled back, Mrs Blackthorn's words hitting her like a physical blow. The room seemed to spin around her, and she gripped the doorframe to steady herself. Tears burned in her eyes, but she refused to let them fall.

"That's not true," Clara whispered, her voice trembling. "Edward is my friend. And my singing... it's not frivolous. It's who I am."

Mrs Blackthorn sneered. "Who you are? You're an orphan, Clara. Nothing more. The sooner you accept that, the better off you'll be."

Clara's chest tightened, each breath a struggle. She wanted to scream, to argue, to make Mrs Blackthorn understand. But the words wouldn't come. Instead, she turned and fled, her footsteps echoing in the empty hallway.

She ran until she reached the small alcove beneath the stairs, her secret hiding place. There, in the dusty darkness, Clara finally let her tears fall. She hugged her knees, her body shaking with silent sobs.

As the minutes ticked by, Clara's tears gradually subsided. She wiped her eyes with the back of her hand, taking a deep, shuddering breath. In the quiet of her hiding place, she began to hum softly.

With each note, Clara felt her resolve strengthen. Mrs Blackthorn was wrong. Her voice wasn't frivolous – it was her connection to her parents, to her faith, to everything good in her life.

Clara emerged from her hiding place, her chin held high. She may be an orphan, but that didn't define her. She was Clara Winters, and her voice would not be silenced.

DECORATIONS

~~~~

The scent of pine permeated the air, mingling with the lingering aroma of beeswax candles, as Clara hung the last of the evergreen garlands along the church's stone walls. Now sixteen, her sapphire eyes still held the same spark of wonder they had when she first arrived at St Mary's.

"Mind you don't snag that garland, girl," Mrs Blackthorn's sharp voice cut through Clara's reverie. "We can't afford to waste a single branch."

Clara nodded, carefully adjusting the greenery. "Yes, Mrs Blackthorn," she replied, her voice soft but steady.

As she stepped back to survey her work, Clara couldn't help but feel a flutter of excitement. Tonight was the Christmas Eve service, and she would be singing a solo. It was an opportunity to share her gift, one she cherished despite Mrs Blackthorn's constant reminders that it was a "frivolous pursuit."

All around her, the church buzzed with activity. Younger children scurried about, hanging paper snowflakes and setting out hymn books. The air crackled with anticipation and nervous energy.

Mrs Blackthorn prowled the aisles, her critical gaze missing nothing. "You there," she barked at a small boy struggling with a candle holder. "Be careful with that! We can't afford to replace it if you break it."

Clara winced at the harshness in the headmistress's tone, but kept her focus on her own tasks. How Reverend Thornton had convinced her to allow the orphans to aid in the service, Clara could never guess, but she was extremely grateful to him.

As she moved to the altar to arrange the poinsettias, she caught sight of her reflection in a polished brass candlestick. For a moment, she barely recognised herself – gone was the scared little girl who had arrived at St Mary's all those years ago. In her place stood a young woman, her chin held high despite Mrs Blackthorn's constant disapproval.

As Clara placed the last flower, she allowed herself a small smile. Tonight, she would sing. And for those few precious moments, she would be free.

PRACTISE

The air inside the church was now crisp. Everyone had left now that the preparations were all made, but their warmth would return imminently with the start of the event.

Clara's breath formed small clouds as she made her way to the altar. She had snuck in for one final practise before it all began. The flickering candlelight cast dancing shadows on the walls, creating an almost ethereal atmosphere.

She stood before the altar, clasping her hands together to still their trembling. Clara took a deep breath, closed her eyes, and began to sing. Her voice, clear and pure, filled the cavernous space. The acoustics of the church amplified her melody, wrapping her in a cocoon of sound.

As the last note faded, Clara opened her eyes, a small smile playing on her lips. The empty church had always been her favourite place to practice, away from Mrs Blackthorn's critical gaze and the curious stares of the other orphans.

"That was beautiful," a familiar voice said softly.

Clara turned to see Edward Thornton emerging from the shadows near the organ loft. He had grown tall and lean, his dark hair slightly tousled as if he'd been running his fingers through it.

"Edward," Clara breathed, her cheeks flushing slightly. "I didn't know you were here."

He approached her, a warm smile on his face. "I came early to make sure the organ was in tune. I couldn't help but listen when I heard you singing."

Clara ducked her head, embarrassed but pleased. "I was just practicing for tonight."

"Well, you sound wonderful," Edward said, his brown eyes twinkling. "But if you'd like, we could run through it together. I could accompany you on the organ."

Clara nodded eagerly, and Edward took his place at the organ. As his fingers touched the keys, Clara let the music wash over her, and began to sing.

CLARA'S SOLO

Clara's heart raced as she peeked through the curtain separating the vestry from the main church. The pews filled rapidly with townsfolk and patrons, their excited chatter creating a low hum that reverberated through the stone walls. The air was thick with anticipation and the smell of pine from the freshly cut garlands adorning the altar.

She watched as families settled into their seats, children fidgeting in their Sunday best. The soft glow of candles cast a warm light over the congregation, illuminating faces both familiar and strange. Clara recognised Mrs Thurlson from the bakery, her arms laden with baskets of Christmas treats no doubt to hand out to the children after the service. Mr Falls, the town's most prominent lawyer, sat in the front row, his wife adjusting the ribbons in their daughter's hair.

Clara's gaze drifted to the decorations she and the other orphans had painstakingly arranged. Sprigs of holly and mistletoe adorned the window sills, while a grand Christmas tree stood proudly near the altar, its ornaments twinkling in the candlelight. The sight filled her with a bittersweet mix of pride and longing for the Christmases she once shared with her parents.

As the last of the attendees found their seats, Reverend Thornton made his way to the pulpit. His presence immediately commanded attention, and a hush fell over the crowd. Clara held her breath.

"Welcome, friends and neighbours," Reverend Thornton's warm voice rang out. "On this blessed Christmas Eve, we gather not just to celebrate the birth of our Saviour, but to remind ourselves of the importance of community and charity."

Clara listened intently as he spoke of the hardships many faced and the difference even small acts of kindness could make. Her fingers nervously played with the hem of her sleeve, a hand-me-down that she had altered herself.

"And now," Reverend Thornton continued, a smile evident in his voice, "it is my great pleasure to introduce a very special performance. Many of you have heard her angelic voice in our choir, but tonight, she will be singing a solo."

Clara's heart skipped a beat. This was it.

"Please welcome Miss Clara Winters, whose talent and dedication has been a true blessing to our church."

Clara stepped forward, her heart pounding like a drum beneath her ribs. Countless eyes fell upon her, but she squared her shoulders and lifted her chin. As she took her place before the congregation, she caught sight of Edward at the organ, his encouraging smile a beacon of support.

She took a deep breath, filling her lungs with the crisp, pine-scented air. The first notes of "O Holy Night" flowed from her lips, soft and pure as freshly fallen snow. Her voice, tremulous at first, gained strength with each passing measure.

As Clara sang, the world around her faded away. The flickering candlelight, the sea of faces, even the stone walls of the church melted into the background. There was only the music, swelling within her chest and pouring forth like a river of gold.

Her voice soared to the rafters, filling every corner of the church with its crystalline clarity. The emotion in her song was palpable, each word infused with the depth of her own experiences – the joy of Christmases past, the sorrow of loss, and the faith that burned eternally in her heart.

The congregation sat transfixed, barely daring to breathe lest they break the intricate pattern of music Clara had woven. Even Mrs Blackthorn, seated near the back with a pinched expression, seemed unable to look away.

In the front row, a regal-looking woman leaned forward, her bright green eyes fixed intently on Clara. She watched the young singer with rapt attention, her gloved hands clasped tightly in her lap.

As Clara's voice swelled to the climax of the song, a wave of warmth seemed to wash over the church. The chill of the winter night outside was forgotten, replaced by a sense of peace and unity that touched every heart present.

DECEPTION

~~~

As the final notes of "O Holy Night" faded away, Clara felt as though she were waking from a dream. The church erupted in applause, the sound washing over her like a wave. She blinked, her vision coming back into focus as she took in the sea of faces before her, many with tears glistening in their eyes.

Reverend Thornton approached, his face beaming with pride. "Clara, my dear, that was truly extraordinary," he said, his voice thick with emotion.

From the corner of her eye, Clara saw Edward approaching. His face was alight with excitement, mirroring her own emotions.

"Clara!" he exclaimed. "That was incredible! I've never heard you sing like that before."

Before Clara could respond to either of them, she noticed the regal-looking woman making her way towards them. The woman's bright green eyes were fixed on Clara with an intensity that made her want to shrink back, but she held her ground.

"Reverend Thornton," the woman said, her voice rich and

cultured. "I must speak with you about this remarkable young lady."

Clara's heart raced as she realised who this must be – Lady Havisham, the renowned patron of the arts. She had heard whispers of the lady's influence and generosity, but never imagined she would attract such attention.

Lady Havisham turned to Clara, her eyes sparkling. "My dear, your voice is a gift. A gift that must be nurtured and shared with the world."

Clara felt her cheeks flush with heat. "Thank you, my lady," she managed to whisper.

"Reverend," Lady Havisham continued, "I would like to offer my sponsorship for Clara's musical education. With proper training, I believe she could have a bright future ahead of her."

Clara looked to Reverend Thornton, hardly daring to believe what she was hearing. The reverend's face split into a wide grin.

"Lady Havisham, your generosity is overwhelming," he said. "Clara, what do you think?"

Clara opened her mouth, but no words came out. Her mind whirled with possibilities – a life dedicated to music, free from the constraints of the orphanage, a chance to make her parents proud.

"I... I don't know what to say," she finally stammered. "Thank you, Lady Havisham. This is more than I ever dreamed possible."

Clara's heart soared with hope as Lady Havisham's words sank in. A future filled with music, learning, and opportunity stretched before her like a sunlit path. She glanced at Edward, his eyes shining with excitement for her.

But the moment shattered as Mrs Blackthorn's voice cut through the air, sharp as a knife. "I'm afraid I must object, Lady Havisham."

Clara's stomach dropped. She turned to see Mrs Blackthorn

approaching, her face a mask of concern that didn't quite reach her steely eyes.

"While Clara does possess a lovely voice, I'm afraid her behaviour at St. Mary's has been less than exemplary," Mrs Blackthorn said, her words dripping with false regret.

Clara's mouth fell open in shock. She wanted to protest, but the words stuck in her throat.

Mrs Blackthorn continued, her gaze sweeping from Lady Havisham to Reverend Thornton. "I've caught her in numerous lies, shirking her duties, and even stealing food from the kitchen. It pains me to say this, but Clara has proven herself untrustworthy and rebellious."

Clara felt the blood drain from her face. She looked desperately at Reverend Thornton, silently pleading for him to see through Mrs Blackthorn's lies. But doubt had crept into his kind eyes, and he frowned deeply.

Lady Havisham's expression hardened, her earlier warmth evaporating. "Is this true, child?" she asked, her voice cool and distant.

"No!" Clara finally found her voice, though it came out as a strangled whisper. "I would never—"

But Mrs Blackthorn spoke over her. "I'm sorry to disappoint you, Lady Havisham. I know how much you value honesty and good character in those you sponsor."

Clara's world spun as Mrs Blackthorn's accusations hung in the air. She stared at Reverend Thornton, her eyes wide with desperation. His face, once beaming with pride, now creased with confusion and disappointment.

"No, please," Clara choked out. "It's not true. I've never stolen or lied. I wouldn't—"

Tears spilled down her cheeks, hot and stinging. She wiped at them furiously, trying to compose herself, but the sobs kept coming.

Edward stepped forward, his face flushed with anger. "This

is ridiculous! Clara's the most honest person I know. She wouldn't do any of those things."

Mrs Blackthorn's lips curled into a thin smile. "I'm afraid you don't know her as well as you think, young Master Thornton. I've witnessed her deceit firsthand."

Clara's legs trembled beneath her. She looked to Lady Havisham, hoping to find a shred of understanding in those bright eyes. But the lady's gaze had turned cold, her earlier warmth replaced by stern disapproval.

"I had such high hopes," Lady Havisham said, shaking her head. "But I cannot in good conscience sponsor someone of questionable character."

"Please," Clara begged, her voice cracking. "I've always tried to be good. I would never—"

But Mrs Blackthorn cut her off. "Now, now, Clara. There's no need for more lies. You've brought shame upon yourself and St. Mary's."

Reverend Thornton placed a hand on Clara's shoulder, his touch gentle but his expression grave. "Clara, my dear, I'm deeply disappointed. I thought I knew you better than this."

Clara's heart shattered. She opened her mouth to protest again, but no words came out. She looked at Edward, who stood with his fists clenched, glaring at Mrs Blackthorn.

"This isn't right," Edward insisted. "Father, you can't believe—"

"That's quite enough, Edward," Reverend Thornton said firmly. He turned to Mrs Blackthorn, his shoulders slumped. "What do you propose we do now, Mrs Blackthorn?"

Mrs Blackthorn's eyes glinted with triumph. "I believe it would be best for Clara to be removed from the choir and any public performances. Perhaps some time away from St. Mary's would be beneficial. I know of a household in need of a scullery maid..."

Clara's legs gave way beneath her, and she sank to her knees, her dreams crumbling around her. The warmth and joy she'd felt moments ago during her performance vanished, replaced by a cold, hollow ache.

"The Flint estate will graciously agree to take Clara on as a scullery maid, I'm sure," Mrs Blackthorn announced, her voice dripping with false concern. "It's for the best, really. A change of scenery might help her... reflect on her behaviour."

Clara looked desperately at Reverend Thornton, silently pleading for him to see through Mrs Blackthorn's lies. But his kind eyes were clouded with doubt and disappointment.

"No," Clara whispered. "Please, it's not true. I've never—"

But Mrs Blackthorn spoke over her. "Now, Clara, there's no need for more fabrications. You'll leave for the Flint estate tomorrow morning."

Edward stepped forward, his face flushed with anger. "This is absurd! You can't just send her away like this!"

"Edward," Reverend Thornton said, his voice stern. "I said that's quite enough."

Clara's gaze darted between the faces around her – Mrs Blackthorn's smug satisfaction, Lady Havisham's cool disappointment, Reverend Thornton's conflicted frown. Their judgment pressed down on her, suffocating.

"But what about my singing?" Clara asked, her voice small and broken. "The choir?"

Mrs Blackthorn shook her head and tutted. "I'm afraid those privileges are no longer available to you, Clara. It's time you learned the value of honest work."

Clara's dreams of music and a brighter future shattered like glass. She thought of the hymnal tucked away in her meagre possessions, the only connection to her parents and her passion. Now, even that small comfort would be denied to her.

Tears spilled down Clara's cheeks as the full weight of her

situation crashed over her. She was to be sent away, alone, to a strange place, branded a liar and a thief. And worst of all, she'd lost the trust and support of those she'd come to care for.

GOODBYES

Clara sat on her thin mattress, her trembling hands folding the few dresses she owned. The dormitory, usually filled with chatter and movement, had fallen eerily quiet. Only the soft rustle of fabric and the occasional sniffle broke the silence.

She reached for her hymnal, running her fingers over its worn leather cover. Memories flooded her mind – singing with her parents, the joy of performing in the choir, Edward's encouraging smile. Clara clutched the book to her chest, fighting back tears.

"Clara?" A timid voice whispered from the next bed. "Is it true? Are you really leaving?"

She looked up to see Lily, one of the younger girls, watching her with wide, sorrowful eyes. Clara nodded, unable to find her voice.

Lily slipped off her bed and padded over, wrapping her arms around Clara's shoulders. "It's not fair," she mumbled into Clara's hair. "You're the best of us. You make everything brighter."

More girls gathered around, their faces etched with concern

and disbelief. Emily, usually so boisterous, spoke in a hushed tone. "We don't believe what Mrs. Blackthorn said. We know you'd never steal or lie."

Clara's throat tightened. "Thank you," she managed to whisper.

Maggie, the oldest girl in the dormitory, stepped forward. In her hand, she held a small, crudely wrapped package. "We... we wanted you to have this," she said, offering it to Clara. "It's not much, but..."

Clara carefully unwrapped the gift to find a handkerchief embroidered with musical notes. The stitching was uneven, clearly done by inexperienced hands, but to Clara, it was beautiful.

"We all worked on it," Maggie explained. "We were planning on giving you this tomorrow, for Christmas, so please don't forget us."

Tears spilled down Clara's cheeks. "Thank you so much. This is one of the kindest things anyone has ever done for me."

The girls surrounded Clara, offering quiet words of comfort and solidarity. Some shared memories of times Clara's singing had lifted their spirits. Others promised to pray for her every night.

As curfew approached, they reluctantly returned to their beds. Clara finished packing her small bag, carefully placing the handkerchief alongside her hymnal. She lay down, staring at the ceiling, her heart heavy with the weight of leaving behind this makeshift family.

FAREWELL PROMISES

Clara stood outside St Mary's Orphanage, her small bag clutched tightly. The cool morning air nipped at her cheeks, but she barely noticed. Her eyes, red-rimmed from a night of silent tears, scanned the empty street for the carriage that would take her away from everything she'd known for the past nine years.

The orphanage loomed behind her, its gray walls seeming even more oppressive than usual. Clara refused to look back, afraid that if she did, her resolve would crumble. Instead, she focused on the hymnal in her bag, its familiar weight a small comfort amidst the turmoil of her emotions.

A figure appeared in the distance, running towards her. Clara's heart leapt as she recognized Edward's lanky frame. His usually neat hair was disheveled, his cheeks flushed from exertion. As he drew closer, Clara could see the worry etched across his face.

"Clara!" Edward called out, his voice cracking slightly. He skidded to a stop in front of her, breathing heavily.

Clara looked up at him, her lips trembling as she fought to maintain her composure. "Edward, I—"

Before she could finish, Edward took her hands in his. His touch was warm, familiar, and Clara felt her carefully constructed walls begin to crumble. Edward's eyes, usually so full of mischief and joy, were now brimming with unshed tears.

"Is it true?" he asked, his voice barely above a whisper. "Are you really leaving? Mrs Blackthorn wasn't just making threats?"

Clara nodded, unable to form words past the lump in her throat. Edward's grip on her hands tightened, as if he could keep her there through sheer force of will.

Clara's lower lip trembled as she looked up at Edward, her blue eyes swimming with unshed tears. "I didn't do it, Edward," Clara's voice cracked. "I swear I didn't steal anything, or do *anything* wrong. Mrs Blackthorn... she's sending me away to work for the Flint family as a scullery maid. She says it's for my own good, but I know she just wants to be rid of me."

Edward's jaw clenched, his eyes flashing with a mixture of anger and determination. He squeezed Clara's hands tightly, his thumbs rubbing small circles on her palms. "I believe you, Clara. Every word. You're the most honest person I know."

Clara felt a small flicker of warmth in her chest at his words, a stark contrast to the cold dread that had settled in her stomach since Mrs Blackthorn's accusation.

"I'll do everything in my power to clear your name," Edward continued, his voice low and fierce. "I'll talk to my father, to Lady Havisham, to anyone who will listen. We'll bring the truth to light, I promise you."

Clara's breath hitched as she fought back a sob. "But what if—"

"No," Edward cut her off gently. "No 'what ifs'. I know you're innocent, and I won't rest until everyone else knows it too. You don't belong at the Flints', Clara. You belong here, singing in the choir, bringing joy to everyone who hears your voice."

His hands tightened around hers, and Clara could feel the strength of his conviction flowing through that simple touch.

For a moment, she allowed herself to hope, to believe that maybe, just maybe, this wasn't the end of her dreams.

She clung to him, her tears soaking into the fabric of his coat. His arms around her felt like a shield against the cruel world that threatened to tear them apart.

"I'll write to you," Edward whispered, his breath warm against her ear. "And you must write back, Clara. Promise me. Write to me when you get all settled in."

Clara nodded against his chest. The thought of those letters, a tangible connection to Edward and the life she was being forced to leave behind, gave her a small spark of comfort.

"I promise," she finally managed.

Edward pulled back slightly, his hands moving to cup her face. His thumbs gently wiped away her tears, the tender gesture nearly undoing Clara all over again.

"And Clara," he said, "don't ever stop singing. No matter what happens at the Flints', no matter how hard things get, promise me you'll keep music in your heart."

Clara met his gaze, seeing the fierce determination in his eyes. She drew strength from it, straightening her shoulders ever so slightly.

"I promise," she said, her voice steadier now. "I'll sing for God and you, Edward. Every day."

Edward smiled, a bittersweet expression that made Clara's heart ache. "And I'll listen for your voice on the wind," he said. "Until we're together again."

Clara closed her eyes, committing this moment to memory – the feel of Edward's hands on her face, the sound of his voice, the feeling of being truly seen and understood. She knew she would need these memories in the dark days ahead.

As they embraced once more, Clara whispered, "Stay strong, Edward. For both of us."

Edward's arms tightened around her. "Always," he murmured. "We'll get through this, Clara. I swear it."

Clara's heart swelled with emotion as Edward gently pulled out of the embrace and reached into his coat pocket. Her eyes widened as he pulled out a folded sheet of paper, its edges slightly crinkled from being carried close to his heart.

"Clara," Edward said, "I want you to have this."

He unfolded the paper carefully, revealing the familiar handwritten notes and lyrics of the song they had composed together. Clara's breath caught in her throat as she recognised their shared creation.

"Our song," she whispered, her fingers trembling as she reached out to touch the paper.

Edward nodded with a bittersweet smile. "I want you to take it with you. Whenever you sing it, think of me. Remember that I'm always supporting you, no matter how far apart we are."

Clara took the sheet music from him, her hands shaking. She pressed it to her heart, feeling as if she could absorb the melody directly into her heart. The paper was warm from Edward's body heat, and she imagined she could feel his presence in every carefully penned note.

"I will," Clara promised. "I'll sing it every day, Edward. It'll be like having a piece of you with me."

She looked down at the music, her eyes tracing the familiar curves of Edward's handwriting mixed with her own. Each note was a memory, each phrase a moment they had shared.

Clara nodded, her eyes meeting Edward's once more. "I'll hold onto this, Edward. It'll be my symbol of hope, my reminder that there's still beauty in the world, even when things seem darkest."

The clatter of hooves on cobblestones caused Clara's heart to sink. The carriage had arrived, far too soon for her liking. She clutched the sheet music tighter, as if it could somehow shield her from the reality of her situation.

Mrs Blackthorn's sharp voice cut through the air. "Miss

Winters! Your transportation has arrived. Come along now, we haven't got all day."

Clara felt Edward stiffen beside her, his jaw clenching at Mrs Blackthorn's cold tone. He placed a gentle hand on Clara's back, guiding her towards the waiting carriage. Each step felt heavier than the last, as if her feet were made of lead.

As they approached the carriage, Clara could feel Mrs Blackthorn's piercing gaze on them. The headmistress stood ramrod straight, her lips pressed into a thin line of disapproval. Clara tried to ignore her, focusing instead on Edward's steady presence beside her.

They reached the carriage door, and Clara knew it was time. She turned to face Edward, her eyes searching his face, trying to memorise every detail. Edward's expression was a mixture of sorrow and determination, his eyes never leaving hers.

"Clara," he said, his voice steady but filled with emotion, "remember, you're never alone. Your music and your faith will always guide you."

Clara nodded. With a deep breath, she turned and stepped up into the carriage, each movement feeling like a farewell to her hopes and dreams.

As she settled onto the hard seat, Clara allowed herself one last look at Edward. He stood tall and proud, his eyes never leaving hers, even as Mrs Blackthorn moved to close the carriage door.

As the carriage pulled away from St Mary's Orphanage, Clara pressed her face against the cold window, her eyes fixed on the figures of Mrs Blackthorn and Edward. The headmistress stood rigid, her arms crossed, a look of grim satisfaction on her face. But it was Edward who held Clara's gaze, his tall form growing smaller with each turn of the carriage wheels.

Clara's heart ached as she watched him raise his hand in a final farewell. She lifted her own hand to the glass, a silent promise passing between them. Even as Edward's figure blurred and faded into the distance, Clara could still feel the warmth of his embrace, hear the determination in his voice.

The carriage rattled along the frost-covered road, each jolt a reminder of the life she was leaving behind. Clara held her small bag, feeling the familiar shape of her hymnal inside. With trembling hands, she pulled it out, along with the precious sheet music Edward had given her.

As the winter landscape rushed by outside, stark and cold, Clara ran her fingers over the well-worn cover of the hymnal. It was more than just a book of songs; it was a lifeline to her past, to the parents she'd lost, to the music that had sustained her through the darkest times at St Mary's.

She unfolded the sheet music carefully, her eyes tracing the notes she and Edward had penned together. Their shared creation seemed to come alive in her hands, each measure a testament to the bond they shared. Clara could almost hear Edward's voice, urging her to keep singing, to hold onto hope.

Despite the sorrow that threatened to overwhelm her, Clara felt a spark of determination ignite in her. She might be leaving behind everything she knew, but she wasn't truly alone. She had her faith, her music, and the memory of Edward's unwavering support.

Clara's resolve strengthened with each mile that passed. Whatever challenges lay ahead, she would face them with courage. She would sing, even if only in whispers, keeping the flame of her passion alive.

SUCH AN OPPORTUNITY

⚜

The carriage rolled to a stop before Flint Manor House. Its ivy-covered walls seeming to stretch endlessly upward; an oppressive chill seemed to emanate from the very stones of the manor.

Clara clutched her small bag tightly, her knuckles white with tension. The driver opened the carriage door, and Clara stepped out onto the gravel drive, her legs unsteady after the journey. The crunch of stone beneath her feet echoed in the eerie silence surrounding the estate.

Tracing the manor's facade with her eyes, Clara took in the rows of dark windows that stared back at her. A shiver ran down her spine, not entirely from the biting winter wind. The gloomy atmosphere felt like a physical weight on her shoulders, threatening to crush the small spark of hope she'd managed to keep alive during the journey.

She swallowed hard, trying to dislodge the lump in her throat. The sheet music Edward had given her crinkled softly in her pocket as she shifted her grip on the bag. The sound was enough to remind her of his parting words. Clara squared her shoulders, drawing strength from the memory of his support and promises.

She forced her feet to move, one step at a time, towards the imposing front door. Each step felt like a battle against an invisible force trying to push her back. But Clara pressed on, her chin lifted in quiet defiance of the manor's gloomy aura.

As she reached the weathered oak door, Clara's hand trembled as she grasped the knocker, its cold metal biting into her palm. Before she could bring it down, the door swung open, revealing two figures that seemed to embody the manor's austere atmosphere.

A stern looking woman stood before her, her angular face set in a stern expression that made Clara's breath catch. This was obviously the housekeeper. Her sharp eyes swept over Clara, seeming to catalogue every imperfection in an instant. Beside her, a large gentleman loomed, his ramrod-straight posture a stark contrast to Clara's travel-weary slouch. The butler of the house.

"I'm Miss Crabtree, the housekeeper here," the woman said, confirming Clara's assumption. "You're late," her voice was as crisp as freshly starched linen. "We expected you an hour ago."

Clara opened her mouth to explain, but the Butler cut her off with a slight clearing of his throat. "My name is Mr Phineas. Your belongings, if you please," he said, extending a gloved hand.

With reluctance, Clara handed over her small bag. Miss Crabtree's lip curled as she peered inside, her brow furrowing at the contents. "Is this all?" she asked, her tone suggesting Clara's possessions were somehow lacking.

Clara nodded, fighting the urge to snatch her bag back and run. Miss Crabtree let out a small "hmph" before turning on her heel. "Follow me," she ordered, her heels clicking sharply on the polished floor.

They led Clara up flights of narrow stairs, past closed doors

THE ORPHAN'S CHRISTMAS HYMN

and hushed corridors, until they reached the attic. Miss Crabtree pushed open a door, revealing a small, sparsely furnished room. A narrow bed, a rickety chair, and a washstand were the only furnishings. The lone window let in a weak, grey light that did little to dispel the gloom.

"This will be your quarters," Miss Crabtree said, her tone leaving no room for argument. "You'll be expected to keep it tidy."

Mr Phineas stepped forward, his face an impassive mask. "Now, to the rules," he began, his voice low and measured. "Punctuality is paramount. You will rise at five each morning, no exceptions. Your duties will be assigned daily, and excellence is the only acceptable standard."

Clara's heart sank as Mr Phineas continued listing the rules, each one feeling like another bar on a cage closing around her. She struggled to keep her face neutral, not wanting to give Miss Crabtree or Mr Phineas any reason to think ill of her on her first day.

"You will address the master and mistress of the house as 'Sir' and 'Madam' at all times," Mr Phineas intoned. "You are to be neither seen nor heard unless called upon. Any breach of these rules will result in immediate dismissal."

Miss Crabtree's eyes narrowed as she added, "And I'll not tolerate any of that singing nonsense I've heard tell of. You're here to work, girl, not warble like some caged bird."

Clara balked at those words. The thought of not being able to sing, even to herself, felt like a physical blow. She opened her mouth to protest, but quickly thought better of it, clamping her lips shut.

Mr Phineas raised an eyebrow at Clara's reaction. "Is that understood, Miss Winters?"

Clara nodded, not trusting her voice to remain steady if she spoke.

"Very well," Miss Crabtree said, her tone clipped. "You'll find your uniform in the wardrobe. Change immediately and come down to the servant's hall. I pointed it out to you on the way up here, do you remember?"

Clara nodded again.

"Good. Now we'll leave you to change." Miss Crabtree said. "Don't be late again."

As they turned to leave, Mr Phineas paused at the door. "One last thing, Miss Winters," he said, his voice softening almost imperceptibly. "Do try to remember that while this may not be the life you expected, it is a respectable position in a good household. Many would be grateful for such an opportunity."

With that, they left, the door closing behind them with a soft click that seemed to echo in the small, bare room.

THE STAFF OF THE FLINT ESTATE

Clara made her way down to the servant's hall, her new uniform feeling stiff and unfamiliar against her skin. The smell of warm food wafted through the air, making her stomach growl softly. She hadn't realised how hungry she was until that moment.

As she entered the hall, Clara's eyes swept over the assembled staff. A plump woman with rosy cheeks stood by the stove, ladling something that smelled delicious into bowls. When she spotted Clara, her face broke into a warm smile.

"Welcome, dear," she said, her voice as warm as fresh-baked bread. "I'm Cook. Well, technically I'm Mabel, but everyone here just calls me Cook! Come, sit down and have some stew. You must be famished after your journey."

A small knot of tension inside Clara loosened at Cook's kindness. She stepped forward, gratefully accepting the bowl of steaming stew.

"Thank you," she murmured, careful to keep her voice low as she remembered Mr Phineas's admonition about being neither seen nor heard.

As Clara took a seat at the long wooden table, she noticed

two young women watching her. One was petite with bright green eyes that sparkled with curiosity as they looked Clara over. The other was taller and sturdier, her posture radiating confidence. Both wore the same uniform as Clara, marking them as fellow housemaids.

"That's Betsy and Mary," Cook said, nodding towards the two women. "Girls, this is Clara. She'll be joining us."

Betsy offered a small nod, her lips quirking into what might have been a smile. Mary, on the other hand, merely inclined her head slightly, her face remaining impassive.

Clara felt her cheeks warm under their scrutiny. She ducked her head, focusing on her stew and trying to ignore their gazes. The rich, savoury broth warmed her from the inside out, but did little to ease the knot of anxiety in her stomach.

Clara looked up from her stew as a tall, lean young man entered the servant's hall. His posture was impeccable, and his dark eyes swept the room with practiced efficiency. When his gaze fell on Clara, he offered a polite nod.

"Good evening," he said, his voice smooth and measured. "You must be Clara. I'm Thomas, the footman."

Clara returned his nod, noting the reserved kindness in his expression. "Pleased to meet you, Thomas," she replied softly.

Thomas gave her a small smile before moving to collect his own bowl of stew. His movements were graceful and purposeful, speaking to years of practice in his role. Clara watched as he took a seat at the far end of the table, maintaining a respectful distance from the others.

Just as Clara was about to return her attention to her meal, the door to the servant's hall creaked open once more. An older man with a weathered face and kind eyes stepped inside, bringing with him the scent of earth and fresh air.

"Evening, all," he said, his voice rough but warm. His eyes crinkled at the corners as he smiled, spotting Clara. "Ah, you must be our new addition."

He made his way over to Clara, extending a calloused hand. "John Weatherby, groundskeeper. But everyone just calls me Old John."

Clara shook his hand, surprised by the gentleness of his grip despite his obvious strength. "Clara Winters, sir. It's nice to meet you."

Old John's smile widened. "Welcome to Flint Manor, Clara. Listen, if you ever need a moment's peace, you're always welcome in the gardens. There's nothing like a bit of fresh air to soothe the soul."

Clara felt a rush of gratitude at his kindness. "Thank you, Mr. Weatherby. I'll keep that in mind."

"John, please," he insisted with a wink. "We're all friends here."

FIRST DAYS

Clara's eyes fluttered open in the darkness, her body tensing as she realised it was time to begin another day of work. She slipped out of bed, the floorboards creaking softly under her feet as she made her way to the washbasin, splashing cold water on her face to chase away the last vestiges of sleep.

As she dressed in her plain uniform, Clara's fingers fumbled with the buttons. Her muscles ached from yesterday's labour, but she pushed the discomfort aside. There was no time for self-pity in this new life.

Clara crept down the narrow servants' staircase, making her way to the kitchen. Cook nodded a silent greeting as Clara set about lighting the fires and preparing for the day's meals. The routine was becoming familiar now, but no less exhausting.

Hours passed in a blur of endless tasks. Clara scrubbed floors until her knees were raw, polished silverware until she could see her reflection in each spoon, and dusted every nook and cranny of the vast manor. All the while, she felt Miss Crabtree's sharp gaze following her every move.

"You missed a spot," Miss Crabtree's voice cut through the

silence, making Clara jump. She looked up to see the housekeeper pointing at a barely visible smudge on the bannister.

"I'm sorry, Miss Crabtree," Clara murmured, reaching for her cloth. "I'll do it again right away."

As Clara re-polished the entire bannister, she caught a glimpse of something in Miss Crabtree's eyes. It wasn't quite approval, but perhaps a flicker of acknowledgment. Clara straightened her back and redoubled her efforts, determined to prove her worth.

Her hands were raw and her body ached, but she held her head high. She had survived her first days at Flint Manor, and she would continue to persevere. As she finished her evening tasks, Clara noticed Miss Crabtree watching her with an appraising look.

"Well done, girl," Miss Crabtree said curtly, before turning on her heel and striding away.

It wasn't much, but to Clara, those two words felt like a hard-won victory.

∽

CLARA'S DAYS at Flint Manor fell into a gruelling routine. She rose before dawn, her muscles protesting as she dressed in her plain uniform. The work never seemed to end – scrubbing floors, polishing silver, dusting every surface until her fingers ached. Yet through it all, Clara rarely caught sight of the master of the house.

Mr Flint was like a ghost, flitting through the corridors when Clara least expected it. She'd catch glimpses of his tall frame disappearing around corners or hear the echo of his footsteps retreating down the hall. He always wore a serious expression, brow furrowed in deep thought.

One afternoon, as Clara polished the banister near Mr

Flint's study, she heard raised voices from within. The door flew open, and Mr Flint strode out, nearly colliding with her.

He barely spared her a glance before hurrying away without a word.

Clara's cheeks burned with embarrassment as she ducked her head and resumed her work. She couldn't help but wonder about the man who owned this grand house yet seemed so removed from it.

Later that evening, as Clara helped Cook prepare dinner, she worked up the courage to ask about Mr Flint.

Cook sighed, her hands never pausing as she kneaded dough. "Mr Flint's always been more interested in his business than anything else. Even when he's home, his mind's on the next deal or investment."

Thomas, the footman, chimed in as he polished glasses nearby. "I've heard he's trying to expand his factories overseas. Spends more time with ledgers and contracts than with people, if you ask me."

Clara nodded, absorbing this information. It explained the distant, preoccupied air Mr Flint carried with him on the rare occasions she saw him. She couldn't help but feel a twinge of sadness for the man who seemed to have everything, yet appeared so isolated.

MRS FLINT

Clara's first week at Flint Manor had been a whirlwind of endless chores and exhaustion, but nothing could have prepared her for the oppressive presence of Mrs Flint. Unlike her elusive husband, Mrs. Flint seemed to materialise around every corner, her cold eyes scrutinising every surface and movement.

On a crisp morning, Clara found herself assigned to clean the drawing room. She approached the task with determination, meticulously dusting each ornate piece of furniture and polishing the windows until they gleamed. As she stepped back to admire her work, a chill ran down her spine at the sound of Mrs Flint's voice behind her.

"I see you've finally decided to make an attempt at proper cleaning," Mrs Flint said, her tone dripping with disdain.

Clara turned, forcing herself to meet the woman's icy gaze. "Yes, ma'am. I've done my best to ensure everything is spotless."

Mrs Flint sneered as she strode across the room, her fingers trailing along surfaces Clara had just cleaned. "Your best? I think not. Look here," she said, pointing to an imaginary speck on a side table. "And these windows – streaked beyond belief. I expected better, even from someone of your... background."

Clara's cheeks burned with humiliation, but she bit her tongue and nodded. "I'll do it again right away, ma'am."

As the days passed, Clara longed for the comfort of Sunday services. The thought of sitting in a pew, surrounded by the familiar hymns and prayers, filled her with a desperate yearning. Gathering her courage, she approached Mrs Flint one evening after dinner.

"Excuse me, Mrs Flint. I was wondering if I might have permission to attend church on Sundays?"

Mrs Flint's eyes narrowed. "Church? On Sundays? I think not. The work of this household doesn't stop for something as frivolous as that."

Clara's heart sank. "But, ma'am, surely just for an hour or two—"

"Enough," Mrs Flint snapped. "You may spend a bit of time reading your Bible in your room if you must, but none in this household attend church regularly. Mr Flint and I only go on holidays when it's socially necessary. That will be all."

LETTERS

◈

Clara's heart leapt when she saw the envelope addressed to her in Edward's neat handwriting. She savoured the moment before carefully opening it. Her eyes devoured every word as she read:

"*Dearest Clara,*

I hope this letter finds you well. Life at St Paul's isn't the same without your voice filling the halls. How are you settling in at the Flint estate? I pray they're treating you kindly.

The choir misses you terribly. Mr Hawthorne keeps saying no one can hit the high notes quite like you could. Father asks after you often and sends his warmest regards.

Please write back soon and tell me everything. Know that you're in my thoughts and prayers always.

Your friend,

Edward"

Clara read the letter three times over, her fingers tracing the words. She closed her eyes, imagining Edward's voice speaking them. For a moment, she was back at St Mary's, laughing with him as they practiced harmonies.

That night, after her chores were done, Clara sat at the small desk in her attic room. By the flickering light of a candle, she poured her heart onto the page:

"*Dear Edward,*

Your letter is a beacon of light in what has been a trying time. The Flint estate is grand, but cold. The work is endless and gruelling. Mrs Flint seems to find fault in everything I do, no matter how hard I try.

I miss the music most of all. There's no singing allowed here, not even humming. Sometimes, when I'm alone, I whisper the words to our favorite hymns. It's not the same, but it helps me feel close to you and the life I left behind.

I dream of the day we can sing together again. Until then, your letters will be my melody.

Your friend always,

Clara"

She sealed the letter with trembling hands, her heart full of hope. As she drifted off to sleep that night, Clara imagined Edward's face lighting up as he read her words, just as hers had when she received his letter.

∼

EDWARD UNFOLDED CLARA'S LETTER. He'd been waiting anxiously for news since her abrupt departure from St Mary's. As he read, his brow furrowed, his chest tightening with each line detailing her struggles at the Flint estate.

He paced his small room, letter clutched to his chest, mind racing with ways to help. The injustice of it all burned in his throat. Clara, with her angelic voice and kind spirit, reduced to scrubbing floors and enduring endless criticism. It wasn't right.

Settling at his desk, Edward pulled out a fresh sheet of paper. His pen hovered for a moment before he began to write, pouring out his heart.

"*My dearest Clara,*

Your letter brought both joy and sorrow. Joy to hear from you at last, but sorrow at the trials you face. Please know that not a day passes when I don't think of you and the music we shared.

I want you to know that I believe in you, Clara. Your talent, your spirit – they're too bright to be dimmed by your current circumstances. Remember the way your voice soared in the church? That gift is still within you, even if you can't sing aloud right now.

Things at St Mary's remain much the same. Mrs Blackthorn is as stern as ever, but I've noticed her watching the choir with a wistful expression lately. Perhaps she misses your voice too, though she'd never admit it.

Father asks after you often. He's been teaching me more about running the parish, but I confess my mind often wanders to our duets at the organ.

Clara, I promise you this: we will meet again. Your dreams aren't lost, merely deferred. Keep hope alive in your heart, as I do in mine. Hum our song when you feel low – I'll be humming it too, thinking of you.

With unwavering faith in you,
Edward"

He read over the letter, hoping his words would bring her some comfort. Folding it carefully, he sealed it with a whispered prayer that it would reach her safely.

CLARA FINDS HER PLACE

The scent of freshly baked bread wafted up from the kitchen, drawing Clara like a siren's call. Her stomach grumbled as she descended the narrow servants' staircase, her bones aching from another day of endless scrubbing and polishing. As she pushed open the heavy wooden door, the warmth enveloped her, a stark contrast to the chill that seemed to permeate the rest of Flint Manor.

Cook stood at the large wooden table, her plump arms dusted with flour as she kneaded another batch of dough. She looked up as Clara entered, her eyes crinkling with a smile that never failed to lift Clara's spirits.

"There you are, dear. Come, sit down before you fall down," Cook said, gesturing to a stool near the hearth.

Clara sank onto the seat gratefully, feeling the heat from the fire seep into her tired muscles. Cook bustled over, wiping her hands on her apron before placing a steaming bowl of stew in front of Clara.

"Eat up now. You're looking far too thin for my liking," Cook tutted, then turned back to her work.

Clara spooned the rich broth into her mouth, savouring each

bite. As she ate, she watched Cook's practiced movements, finding a strange comfort in the rhythmic thump of dough hitting the table.

"Would you like some help, Cook?" Clara asked, setting down her empty bowl.

Cook's eyes twinkled. "I thought you'd never ask. Come on then, wash your hands and you can help me shape these loaves."

Clara did as she was told, then stood beside Cook at the table. Under the older woman's gentle guidance, she began to form the dough into neat ovals. The familiar motions reminded her of baking with her mother, and for a moment, the ache in her heart eased.

"That's it, love. You've got a natural touch," Cook praised, her warm hand patting Clara's shoulder.

As they worked side by side, peace washed over Clara. The kitchen, with its comforting smells and Cook's motherly presence, became a sanctuary from the cold demands of the rest of the house.

∼

CLARA SCRUBBED the floor of the grand hallway, her arms aching from the repetitive motion. She glanced up to see Betsy dusting the ornate gilt-framed mirrors that lined the walls. For weeks, they'd worked side by side in silence, but today, something felt different.

Betsy caught Clara's eye and offered a small smile. "You've got a knack for getting those stubborn stains out," she said softly.

Clara blinked in surprise. "Thank you. I've had plenty of practice," she replied.

Betsy's shoulders relaxed a fraction. "I remember when I first started here. Felt like my arms would fall off every night."

Clara nodded, grateful for the shared experience. "Does it ever get easier?"

"The work? Not really. But you get stronger," Betsy said with a wry grin.

As they continued their tasks, they exchanged quiet words about their lives before Flint Manor. Clara learned that Betsy came from a large family in Manchester, and Betsy listened intently as Clara shared snippets of her time at St Mary's.

"I miss singing," Clara admitted.

Betsy's eyes widened. "You sing? I'd love to hear you someday."

Clara shook her head. "Mrs Flint forbade it."

Betsy frowned. "That's a shame. Maybe... maybe you could sing for us in the servants' hall sometime? When the Flints are out?"

Clara felt a spark of hope ignite within her. "I'd like that."

Later that afternoon, as Clara polished silverware in the kitchen, Mary bustled in, her arms full of linens.

"Here, let me help," Clara offered, reaching for a stack of napkins.

Mary hesitated, then smiled. "Thanks, Clara. You're a quick study, aren't you?"

As they folded the linens together, Mary began to share tips on navigating the household hierarchy. "Always defer to Mr Phineas in front of the family, but if you need something done quickly, go to Miss Crabtree," she advised.

Clara soaked up the information, grateful for Mary's guidance. As they worked, their conversation flowed more freely, touching on their hopes for the future.

"I'd love to run my own boarding house someday," Mary confided.

Clara's eyes lit up. "That sounds wonderful. I... I dream of teaching music to children."

Mary squeezed Clara's hand. "Don't give up on that dream, Clara. You never know what might happen."

∼

Clara noticed a change in Thomas's behaviour as the weeks went by. Though he maintained his professional distance, she caught glimpses of kindness in his actions. One afternoon, as she struggled with a heavy bucket of water for scrubbing the entrance hall, Thomas appeared at her side.

"Allow me, Miss Winters," he said politely. He effortlessly lifted the bucket and carried it to where she needed it.

"Thank you, Thomas," Clara replied, surprised by his assistance.

Thomas gave a quick nod and a fleeting smile before returning to his duties. Clara smiled back, grateful for the small act of kindness.

As the days passed, Clara began to notice more of these subtle gestures. When Miss Crabtree assigned her to polish the silver, a task that always left her arms aching, she found Thomas had already laid out the polishing cloths and arranged the pieces for easier access.

During a particularly trying day when Mrs Flint had been especially critical, Clara caught Thomas's eye as she hurried down the servant's staircase. He offered her a reassuring smile, brief but genuine, that lifted her spirits more than she expected.

Clara understood the delicate balance of the household hierarchy and appreciated Thomas's discretion. He never overstepped his bounds or drew attention to his acts of kindness, but she sensed a depth of empathy beneath his reserved exterior.

One evening, as Clara finished her chores in the kitchen, she overheard Cook speaking to Thomas.

"You're a good lad, Thomas," Cook said warmly. "I've seen how you look out for our Clara."

"I'm sure I don't know what you mean," Thomas replied, his tone neutral but not unkind.

Clara smiled to herself, touched by the unspoken support. She resolved to find a way to thank Thomas, even if only with a grateful glance or a quiet word of appreciation. In the harsh world of Flint Manor, these small kindnesses were a balm to her weary spirit.

∼

Clara relished the rare free afternoon, her feet carrying her towards the sprawling gardens of Flint Manor. The sun warmed her face as she wandered among the carefully tended flowerbeds and neatly trimmed hedges. In the distance, she spotted a gnarled oak tree, its massive branches reaching towards the sky. As she approached, she noticed Old John, his weathered hands gently pruning the lower branches.

"Afternoon, Miss Clara," Old John called out, his eyes crinkling with a warm smile. "Care to join an old man for a spell?"

Clara nodded eagerly, settling onto a nearby bench. "I'd love to, Mr Weatherby."

Old John chuckled, shaking his head. "Now, none of that 'Mr. Weatherby' business. Old John's what everyone calls me, and it suits me just fine."

As Clara watched, Old John's gnarled fingers worked deftly, tending to the ancient oak with a practiced touch. His voice, rich with the accent of his rural upbringing, wove tales of the estate's history and his own life.

"This old tree's been here longer than any of us," he mused. "Seen more summers and winters than I can count. Why, I remember when it was struck by lightning back in '62. Thought for sure we'd lose her, but she's a stubborn one."

Clara listened, enraptured by Old John's stories. He spoke of harsh winters and bountiful harvests, of the changing seasons and the cycles of nature. His words painted vivid pictures of a world beyond the confining walls of Flint Manor.

"You know, Miss Clara," Old John said, his voice taking on a gentler tone, "life's a bit like this old oak. Sometimes it gets battered and bruised, but if you've got strong roots, you'll weather any storm."

Clara felt a lump form in her throat, touched by the wisdom in his words. She found herself opening up, sharing snippets of her own story – of the orphanage, of her love for music, of the hardships she faced in the manor.

Old John listened patiently, nodding in understanding. "You've got a strong spirit, Miss Clara. Don't you ever let anyone dim that light of yours."

As the afternoon waned, Clara reluctantly rose to leave, her heart lighter than it had been in months. "Thank you, Old John," she said softly. "May I... may I come visit you again?"

Old John's face crinkled into a warm smile. "Any time, Miss Clara. Any time at all."

EARNING RESPECT

"Miss Winters, I expect those banisters to shine like mirrors," Miss Crabtree's clipped voice rang out as Clara worked her way down the grand staircase.

Clara bit her lip, focusing on the task at hand. "Yes, Miss Crabtree," she murmured, redoubling her efforts.

Over time, Clara noticed a subtle shift in Miss Crabtree's demeanour. The housekeeper's criticisms, while still frequent, lost some of their biting edge. Once, Clara even caught a flicker of something akin to approval in Miss Crabtree's eyes as she inspected a freshly polished silver service.

But the fragile peace shattered one fateful afternoon. Clara, balancing a tray of delicate china, stumbled on a loose floorboard. The crash echoed through the hallway, shards of porcelain scattering across the floor.

Miss Crabtree appeared in an instant, her face thunderous. "Miss Winters! Your clumsiness knows no bounds!"

Clara's heart pounded as she dropped to her knees, frantically gathering the broken pieces. "I'm so sorry, Miss Crabtree," she said, her voice trembling. "It was an accident. I'll clean it up right away and work extra hours to make up for the loss."

Miss Crabtree opened her mouth, no doubt to deliver a scathing rebuke, but something in Clara's earnest face gave her pause. The girl's hands shook as she carefully collected each shard, but her eyes were filled with determination.

For a long moment, silence reigned. Then, Miss Crabtree's shoulders relaxed ever so slightly. "See that you do, Miss Winters," she said, her tone firm but lacking its usual venom. "I expect this mess to be cleared and the hallway spotless within the hour."

"Yes, Miss Crabtree," Clara nodded, relief flooding through her. "It will be done."

As Miss Crabtree turned to leave, Clara caught a fleeting expression on the housekeeper's face. It wasn't quite approval, but there was a glimmer of something – perhaps respect – in her eyes.

∼

CLARA ADJUSTED the placement of the silver candlesticks on the dining room sideboard. She could feel Mr Phineas's gaze upon her, scrutinising her every move. The butler's presence loomed large in the room, his impeccable posture a stark reminder of the exacting standards expected in the Flint household.

"A quarter-inch to the left, Miss Winters," Mr Phineas intoned, his voice crisp and devoid of emotion.

Clara complied without a word, her fingers carefully nudging the heavy silver piece into place. She held her breath as Mr Phineas leaned in, his eyes narrowing as he inspected her work.

After what felt like an eternity, Mr Phineas straightened up. "Acceptable," he declared, the faintest hint of approval in his voice.

Clara's heart soared at the rare compliment, if it could even be called that. She'd learned quickly that Mr Phineas's "acceptable" was high praise indeed.

As the days passed, Clara studied Mr Phineas's habits and preferences with the same intensity he applied to his duties. She noticed how he preferred the curtains drawn to precisely three-quarters open during the day, how he insisted on a specific fold for the dinner napkins, and the exact angle at which he liked the chairs arranged around the dining table.

One morning, as Clara polished the library's mahogany shelves, she heard Mr Phineas's measured footsteps approaching. Without a word, she adjusted her technique, using the circular motion she'd observed him demonstrating to Thomas the week before.

Mr Phineas paused in the doorway, his eyebrow raised a fraction of an inch as he watched her work. Clara continued her task, her movements steady and precise.

"Very good, Miss Winters," Mr Phineas said softly, the barest nod accompanying his words.

Clara felt a rush of pride at the quiet acknowledgment. She'd earned a moment of Mr Phineas's respect, and in the world of service, that was no small feat.

END OF DAY

The floorboards creaked beneath Clara's feet as she entered the small space she now called home. Moonlight filtered through the single window, casting long shadows across the sparse furnishings.

With a weary sigh, Clara sat on her bed and reached for the worn leather hymnal tucked beneath her pillow. Her fingers traced the embossed letters on its cover, a tangible link to her past. Beside it lay the sheet music Edward had given her, the pages slightly crinkled from frequent handling.

Clara opened the hymnal, humming softly as she read the familiar words. The melody rose and fell, barely audible even in the quiet of her room. It was a silent promise to herself, to Edward, to all those she'd left behind at St Mary's – a vow to keep her spirit and her music alive, no matter the circumstances.

As she sang, Clara felt the day's trials begin to lift. The ache in her muscles eased, and the worries that clouded her mind began to dissipate. In these precious moments, she wasn't just a lowly maid. She was Clara Winters, the girl with the voice that could move hearts.

Setting aside the hymnal, Clara reached for Edward's latest letter. She unfolded it carefully, a smile playing on her lips as she read his words once more. Edward's steadfast friendship and unwavering belief in her talent were beacons of hope in her new life.

Clara took out a sheet of paper and began to write her reply. Her pencil scratched softly against the paper as she described her days at the Flint residence – the challenges she faced, but also the small victories. She wrote of the kindness she'd found in unexpected places: Cook's motherly warmth, Old John's wise counsel, Thomas's quiet support, and even Mr Phineas's grudging approval.

As she wrote, Clara realised that despite the hardships, she was finding her footing in this new world. The friendships she was forging with the household staff, though different from what she'd known before, were becoming a source of strength and comfort.

NO PLACE FOR A MELODY

The music room, with its high ceilings and ornate furnishings, felt like a sanctuary. Here, surrounded by instruments and sheet music, Clara could almost pretend she was back in the church choir. Her fingers glided over the polished surface of the grand piano, her cloth moving in rhythmic circles.

Without realising it, she began to hum a familiar hymn. The melody rose and fell, filling the room with its gentle cadence. Clara's voice grew stronger, the words forming on her lips as she lost herself in the song.

"For the beauty of the earth,
For the beauty of the skies,
For the love which from our birth

Over and around us lies..."

For a moment, she wasn't a lowly maid in a grand house, but simply Clara Winters, the girl with the voice that could touch hearts.

Suddenly, the door burst open with a bang that made Clara jump. Mrs Flint stood in the doorway, her face a mask of irritation. Clara's voice died in her throat, the last notes of the hymn hanging in the air between them.

"What do you think you're doing?" Mrs Flint's voice was sharp, cutting through the lingering echoes of Clara's song.

Clara fumbled with her cleaning cloth, her heart racing. "I... I was just cleaning the piano, ma'am."

"Cleaning? That sounded more like caterwauling to me." Mrs Flint stepped into the room. "Let me make something very clear, girl. There will be no singing in my presence. Do you understand?"

Clara nodded, her throat tight. "Yes, ma'am."

"Singing is a frivolous waste of time and effort," Mrs. Flint continued, her voice dripping with disdain. "You're here to work, not to entertain yourself with silly tunes."

Clara stood frozen, her mind whirling. How could something that brought such joy be considered frivolous? How could the music that had sustained her through so much hardship be dismissed so easily?

"Besides," Mrs Flint's eyes glinted, "I have another task for you."

～

Clara's fingers trembled as she gripped the rough-bristled brush, her knuckles white with cold. The attic air bit at her skin, seeping through the thin fabric of her dress. She knelt on the hard wooden floor, scrubbing at a particularly stubborn stain that refused to yield.

The wind howled outside, finding its way through every

crack and crevice of the old mansion. Clara's teeth chattered, but she pressed on, determined to finish her task.

"Still not done?" Mrs Flint's voice cut through the silence, sharp as the winter air.

Clara looked up, her eyes watering from the dust and the chill. "I'm almost finished, ma'am."

Mrs Flint's lips curled into a sneer. "Almost isn't good enough. When you're done here, the west wing needs attention. Every window must be spotless before nightfall."

Clara's heart sank. The west wing was even colder than the attic, its windows crusted with years of grime. But she nodded, keeping her voice steady. "Yes, ma'am."

As Mrs Flint turned to leave, she paused at the door. "And Clara? I expect silence while you work. No humming, no singing. Is that clear?"

"Yes, ma'am," Clara repeated, her voice barely above a whisper.

Left alone once more, Clara returned to her task. Her hands, red and raw from endless scrubbing, protested with every movement. But she pushed through the pain, focusing on each stroke of the brush.

In her mind, she could hear the faint echo of a hymn, a melody that had once brought her such comfort. Now, it was nothing more than a memory, locked away where Mrs Flint couldn't reach it.

INTERCEPTION

*B*eatrice Flint stalked through the hallways of her manor, her heels clicking against the polished floor. The sound echoed her irritation, each step fueled by the memory of that wretched girl's voice. How dare she sing in her house? The very thought of it made Beatrice's blood boil.

As she rounded the corner, a flash of white caught her eye. There, on the small table where outgoing mail was placed, sat an envelope. Beatrice's eyes narrowed as she recognised the neat, precise handwriting. Clara.

She snatched up the letter, her fingers trembling with anger and anticipation. Without a second thought, she retreated to her private sitting room, locking the door behind her.

Beatrice held the envelope up to the light, studying it. With practiced ease, she carefully opened it, ensuring no trace of tampering would be visible. As she unfolded the letter, her eyes devoured the words, a sneer curling her lips.

"Dearest Edward," it began. Beatrice's grip tightened on the paper, crinkling its edges. She read on, her face hardening with each line of hope, each expression of longing for music and a better life.

"This simply won't do," Beatrice muttered. She stood, letter in hand, and crossed to the fireplace. With a flick of her wrist, she tossed the paper into the flames, watching with grim satisfaction as Clara's words curled and blackened.

In that moment, Beatrice made a decision. No more of Clara's letters would leave this house, and none of Edward's would be delivered to her. Beatrice would crush this girl's spirit, extinguish that insufferable light in her eyes. Clara would learn her place, and Beatrice would ensure she stayed there.

Over the next weeks, Beatrice kept a keen eye on the mail table. Each time she found a letter from Clara or Edward, she repeated the ritual. She read each one, her jealousy and resentment growing with every word of the two's unwavering hope and determination. And each time, she destroyed the evidence, leaving no trace of her interference.

WEATHERING THE STORM

"Here, let me help with that corner," Betsy whispered, kneeling beside Clara. Her gentle eyes held a mix of concern and sympathy. Mrs Flint had assigned Clara yet another extra task, seemingly determined to work her to the bone.

"Thank you," Clara murmured, grateful for the brief respite.

Mary appeared with fresh water, her practical nature shining through. "I've got the next room ready for you, Clara. Don't worry, I've already dusted the high shelves."

Clara was so grateful for her friends. Their small acts of kindness were a balm to her weary spirit.

Later, as they folded linens together, Betsy leaned in close. "I don't understand why Mrs Flint's taken such a dislike to you. Especially about your singing."

Mary nodded, her brow furrowed. "It's not right, the way she treats you. But we've got your back, Clara."

Clara's throat tightened with emotion. "I don't know what I'd do without you both."

As Clara carried a heavy tray of polished silver, she caught

Thomas's eye. He offered a reassuring smile and a subtle nod, his quiet support evident even from across the room.

That evening, Clara escaped to the gardens, finding solace in Old John's company. He took one look at her drawn face and patted the bench beside him.

"Sit a spell, lass. You look like you could use a breather."

Clara sank down gratefully, her body sagging with exhaustion.

"Mrs Flint giving you a hard time again?" Old John asked, his voice gruff but kind.

Clara nodded, unable to find the words.

"You've got more strength in you than you know," he said, patting her hand. "Just remember, even the toughest winter can't stop spring from coming."

His words warmed Clara's heart, giving her the strength to face another day. As she returned to the house, she held her head high, determined not to let Mrs Flint's cruelty break her spirit.

∼

"I JUST DON'T UNDERSTAND," Clara murmured to herself, setting down a freshly polished candlestick.

"What's that?" Betsy asked, looking up from her own work nearby.

Clara hesitated, then sighed. "It's Mrs Flint. The way she reacts when I sing... it's as if I've committed some terrible crime."

Mary glanced around, ensuring they were alone before leaning in. "It is odd, isn't it? You'd think she'd appreciate a bit of music in this gloomy old house."

"Maybe she's tone-deaf," Betsy suggested with a wry smile.

Clara shook her head. "No, it's more than that. It's like she takes it personally."

The girls fell silent as footsteps approached, but it was only Thomas passing by with a laden tray.

Once he'd gone, Mary spoke again. "You know, I've heard whispers from some of the older staff. They say Mrs Flint wasn't always... well, Mrs Flint."

Betsy's eyes widened. "What do you mean?"

Mary glanced at Clara, then back to Betsy. "Perhaps we shouldn't..."

But Clara's curiosity was piqued. "Please, Mary. If there's something that might help me understand..."

Mary sighed, then nodded. "Alright, but keep your voices down. I overheard Cook talking to Old John the other day. Apparently, Mrs Flint had dreams of being a singer when she was younger."

Clara's hands stilled on the silver. "A singer?"

"Yes, and I heard Cook say" Mary excitedly continued, "that it was a terrible shame, really, she had real promise so I heard.

"And then Old John spoke about a disastrous performance, happening in front of a load of people."

"Do you think..." Clara began, but she couldn't finish the thought.

DOUBT CREEPS IN

⊱⊰

The flickering candlelight cast long shadows across the worn wood, mirroring the dark thoughts that crept into Clara's mind. She sat at the small desk in her attic room, quill poised over a fresh sheet of paper, losing count of how many letters she'd written to Edward over the past months. Each one was filled with more desperation than the last.

Her hand trembled slightly as she began to write.

"*Dearest Edward,*

I hope this letter finds you well. It's been so long since I've heard from you, and I can't help but worry. Are you alright? Has something happened?"

Clara paused, biting her lip. She wanted to pour out her fears, her loneliness, but she held back. Instead, she dipped her quill and continued.

"*Life at the Flint estate remains much the same. The work is hard, but I'm managing. I think of you often, especially when I catch a moment to hum a tune. It reminds me of the times we sang together.*"

She hesitated again, then added, "*I miss those days terribly.*"

Clara's eyes stung with tears as she signed her name at the

bottom of the letter. She folded it carefully, sealing it with a drop of wax.

As she prepared for bed, Clara's mind raced with possibilities. Perhaps Edward had fallen ill, or his father had taken a turn for the worse. Maybe he'd been sent away to school and hadn't had a chance to write. Or... Clara's heart clenched at the thought... maybe he had simply forgotten about her.

No, she told herself firmly. Edward wouldn't do that. He had promised to write, to help clear her name. He wouldn't abandon her. Yet as the days stretched into weeks without a reply, doubt began to creep in.

∽

EDWARD SAT at his small desk. The scratching of his pen against paper filled the quiet room as he composed yet another letter to Clara. Sunlight filtered through the dusty window, illuminating the scattered sheet music and dog-earned hymnals that covered every available surface.

"*My dearest Clara,*" he wrote, his brow furrowed with worry. "*I hope this letter finds you well. Your silence these past months has been most concerning. I pray that you are in good health and that my previous correspondence has reached you safely.*"

Edward paused, tapping the pen against his chin. He longed to pour out his heart, to tell Clara how much he missed her voice and her presence. But he tempered his words, knowing that propriety demanded restraint.

"*I continue to think of you often,*" he continued, "*especially when I'm at the church organ. The hymns we used to sing together echo in my mind, and I find myself imagining your voice soaring above the congregation.*"

He described his latest efforts to clear Clara's name, detailing conversations with Reverend Thornton and attempts to reach out to Lady Havisham. "*I remain convinced of your innocence,*" Edward wrote firmly, "*and I will not rest until the truth is known.*"

As he wrote, Edward's mind wandered to their shared dreams of music. He recalled Clara's radiant smile as she sang, the way her eyes lit up when she mastered a difficult piece. "*I've been working on a new composition,*" he added, hoping to spark her interest. "*It's a choral piece inspired by the Psalms. I long for the day when we might perform it together.*"

Edward signed the letter with a flourish, sealing it carefully. He would post it still clinging to the hope that this time, Clara would respond.

Little did Edward know that his heartfelt words would never reach their intended recipient. Miles away, in the opulent study of Flint Manor, Beatrice Flint held Edward's latest letter over a candle flame. She watched with cold satisfaction as the paper curled and blackened, Edward's earnest sentiments disappearing into ash.

"Another one for the fire," Mrs Flint muttered, a cruel smile playing at her lips. She imagined Clara waiting in vain for word from Edward, and Edward growing increasingly desperate at Clara's apparent silence. The thought filled her with a vindictive pleasure.

LOSS

⤞

The gleaming surface reflected Clara's pale face, dark circles forming under her once-bright eyes. She barely registered the clink of spoons as she mechanically moved from one piece to the next.

"Clara?" Thomas's voice startled her. She looked up, realising she'd been polishing the same fork for minutes. "You alright?"

Clara forced a weak smile. "Of course. Just... lost in thought."

Thomas frowned but nodded, leaving her to her work. Clara's shoulders slumped as she returned to her task, the silence pressing down on her.

In the kitchen, she moved like a ghost, chopping vegetables without her usual hum. Cook's concerned gaze followed her, but Clara couldn't bring herself to meet those kind eyes.

"Here, love," Cook said, sliding a warm roll across the table. "You're looking peaky."

Clara murmured her thanks, but the bread tasted like ash in her mouth. She choked it down, knowing she needed the strength to face another day of endless chores and crushing loneliness.

As she scrubbed the floor later, Clara's movements grew

slower, her arms heavy with more than just physical exhaustion. Betsy appeared beside her, wordlessly taking up a brush to help.

"You don't have to—" Clara began, but Betsy cut her off with a gentle smile.

"We look out for each other here," she said softly. "Even when we can't say much."

Tears pricked Clara's eyes, but she blinked them back. She couldn't afford to break down, not here, not now.

Later, as Clara trudged up the stairs with a basket of linens, Mary intercepted her.

"Let me take that," Mary insisted, her voice unusually gentle. "You look done in."

Clara relinquished the basket, her arms aching with relief. "Thank you," she whispered.

Mary hesitated, then squeezed Clara's hand. "Whatever's troubling you, it won't last forever. You're stronger than you know."

The kindness in Mary's eyes nearly undid Clara. She nodded quickly and hurried away, afraid that if she stayed a moment longer, she'd crumble entirely.

∽

EDWARD'S HAND trembled slightly as he began to write, "*My dearest Clara...*" The words felt hollow now, a far cry from the eager anticipation that had once filled him when penning his thoughts to her. As he continued, his usually flowing script became more erratic, betraying the turmoil within.

"*I find myself at a loss,*" he wrote, the ink blotting where his quill lingered too long. "*Your silence weighs heavily upon me. Have you forgotten our friendship? The music we shared?*"

Edward paused, closing his eyes as memories of Clara's angelic voice filled his mind. The joy that had once accompanied these recollections now twisted into a painful ache in his chest.

He crumpled the unfinished letter, tossing it aside. Rising from his chair, Edward moved to the small piano in the corner of his room. His fingers ghosted over the keys, but the melodies that once flowed so easily from his touch now felt discordant and lifeless.

Edward attempted to play a hymn he and Clara had often sung together, but the notes rang flat and uninspired. He stopped abruptly, the sudden silence more deafening than the music had been.

"Why, Clara?" he whispered to the empty room. "Why won't you answer?"

The questions that had plagued him for weeks now rose to the surface, impossible to ignore. Had she found a new life at the Flint estate, one that didn't include him? Had she decided that their friendship was better left in the past?

Edward's shoulders slumped as he closed the piano lid. The instrument that had once been his solace now stood as a painful reminder of what he feared he had lost.

∼

CLARA SAT on the edge of her narrow bed, holding the worn piece of paper. The dim light from the small window cast long shadows across the attic room, mirroring the darkness that had settled in her heart. She read Edward's words for what felt like the hundredth time, each sentence a bittersweet reminder of a friendship that now seemed lost to her.

"*My dearest Clara*," the letter began. The familiar handwriting, once a source of comfort, now felt like a knife twisting in her chest. Clara's vision blurred as fresh tears welled up and spilled down her cheeks.

She traced her fingers over the words, remembering the day

she'd received this letter. It had been full of hope, promises of continued correspondence, and assurances of his unwavering belief in her innocence. But as the weeks had turned into months, and the months into a year without another word from Edward, that hope had withered and died.

Clara's shoulders shook with silent sobs. Her isolation pressed down on her, threatening to crush what little spirit she had left. She had clung to the belief that Edward, of all people, would stand by her. His silence felt like the cruelest betrayal.

"Why, Edward?" she whispered. "Why did you forget me?"

The silence of the attic seemed to mock her. Clara curled up on her bed, clutching the letter. She closed her eyes, trying to recall the sound of Edward's voice, his smile. But even these memories were beginning to fade, replaced by the cold reality of her current existence.

As night fell and the attic grew darker, Clara lay there, her tears slowly drying on her cheeks. The pain of believing she had been abandoned by Edward, the one person who had given her hope and strength, was almost more than she could bear. In that moment, alone in the darkness, Clara felt truly and utterly forsaken.

∽

EDWARD SAT AT THE PIANO, his fingers hovering over the ivory keys. The once-familiar instrument now felt like a stranger, cold and unyielding beneath his touch. He stared at the sheet music before him, the notes blurring into meaningless symbols.

Clara's face floated in his mind, her smile as bright as he remembered from their days at St Mary's. He could almost hear her voice, clear and pure, singing the hymns they'd practiced together. But the memory faded, replaced by the harsh reality of her silence.

Edward's hand fell to his side, unable to bring himself to

play. The music that had once connected them now seemed to mock him, a constant reminder of what he'd lost. He closed his eyes, trying to summon the determination that had driven him for so long.

"Why won't you write back, Clara?" he whispered to the empty room.

The question hung in the air, unanswered. Edward had sent letter after letter, each one filled with reassurances of his belief in her innocence, updates on his life, and pleas for her to respond. But as the weeks turned to months, and the months to a year, his hope had begun to waver.

He stood up abruptly, pacing the room. The possibility that Clara had simply moved on with her life at the Flint estate began to take root in his mind. Perhaps she'd found new friends, new interests. Perhaps she no longer needed the connection to her past that he represented.

Edward's steps slowed as realisation settled on him. He returned to the piano bench, slumping down with a heavy sigh. The sheet music stared back at him.

His fingers traced the edges of the keys, but he couldn't bring himself to play. The music that had once flowed so easily between them now felt like a painful reminder of what was lost. Edward sat there, surrounded by silence, as the last embers of his hope flickered and faded.

THE FINAL BLOW

Clara's footsteps whispered across the dewy grass as she slipped through the darkening gardens of Flint Manor. The day's toil weighed heavy on her shoulders, but a flicker of anticipation sparked in her heart. She'd discovered this hidden nook weeks ago, a small clearing nestled between an ancient oak and a thick tangle of rhododendrons. Old John had shown it to her, a secret shared between them.

The air grew cooler as night settled in, carrying the sweet scent of late-blooming flowers. Clara glanced over her shoulder, ensuring she wasn't followed. The manor's windows glowed with warm light, but from here, it seemed a world away.

She settled onto a smooth, flat stone, worn by years of wind and rain. Clara closed her eyes, taking a deep breath. The silence of the garden enveloped her, broken only by the gentle rustling of leaves and the distant call of a nightingale.

Clara opened her mouth, her voice barely a whisper at first. The words of an old hymn, one her mother had taught her, tumbled from her lips. Her voice trembled, raw with emotion and disuse. She hadn't truly sung in so long, the sound of it almost startled her.

As the familiar melody took shape, Clara's voice grew stronger. The song spoke of hope in dark times, of faith that endures. Tears pricked at her eyes, but she didn't stop. She poured her longing, her fears, and her desperate hope into every note.

The hymn floated on the night air, a fragile thing born of a battered spirit. Yet as Clara sang, something within her began to stir. The music, long suppressed, flowed through her, bringing with it a glimmer of the joy she'd once known.

∼

Beatrice Flint stood by the window of her drawing room, a cup of tea cooling in her hand as she watched Clara trudge across the grounds. The girl's shoulders slumped, her steps heavy with her duties and, Beatrice knew, the crushing disappointment of unanswered correspondence.

A smile tugged at the corners of Beatrice's mouth. She savoured the sight of Clara's dejected posture, a stark contrast to the bright-eyed, singing creature who had first arrived at Flint Manor. Beatrice took a sip of her tea, relishing the bitter taste that matched her satisfaction.

Later that afternoon, Beatrice made her way to her private study. She locked the door behind her and approached a small writing desk tucked away in the corner. With practiced movements, she opened a hidden compartment and extracted a bundle of letters.

Beatrice's fingers traced the familiar handwriting on the envelopes. Some bore Clara's neat script, others the bolder hand of that Thornton boy. She fanned them out before her, a physical representation of her power over Clara's world.

As she read through the latest letter from Edward, Beatrice sneered. The boy's words dripped with concern and affection, sentiments that Clara would never see. Beatrice crumpled the paper in her fist, feeling a rush of vindictive pleasure.

She tossed the letter into the fireplace, watching as the flames devoured Edward's declarations of friendship and promises of support. The sight of the paper blackening and curling filled Beatrice with a perverse joy.

Beatrice returned to her desk, pulling out her personal stationary. She began to compose a letter in a passable imitation of Clara's handwriting. In it, she crafted a life of contentment and new friendships for Clara at Flint Manor, one that left no room for old attachments.

As she sealed the envelope, Beatrice felt a surge of triumph. This, she thought, would be the final blow to whatever lingering hope Edward might harbour. She had become the architect of Clara's isolation, sculpting the girl's emotional landscape to her liking.

THE NAIL IN THE COFFIN

*E*dward couldn't shake the nagging worry that had taken root in his chest. His father, once a pillar of strength and vitality, now moved through the rectory with a sluggishness that set Edward's teeth on edge. The sound of Reverend Thornton's cough echoed through the halls.

"Father, perhaps you should rest," Edward suggested, watching the older man struggle to button his coat.

Reverend Thornton waved him off. "Nonsense, my boy. There's work to be done."

But Edward couldn't ignore the tremor in his father's hands or the pallor that had crept into his once-ruddy cheeks. As the days wore on, he found himself taking on more of his father's duties, stepping in to lead prayers when the Reverend's voice gave out, organising the church accounts when his father's eyes grew too tired to focus on the ledgers.

One crisp autumn morning, as Edward sorted through the mail, his heart leapt at the sight of Clara's handwriting. He tore open the envelope, hope blooming in his chest.

But as he read, that hope withered and died.

"*My dear Edward,*" the letter began, its tone as cold as the first frost. "*I hope this letter finds you well. Life at the Flint Estate has been most agreeable. I find I have everything I need here and have no desire to return to my former life.*"

Edward's hands shook as he read on, each word a dagger to his heart.

"*I must ask that you cease your correspondence. I have no further need of your friendship or concern. Please do not write again.*"

The letter slipped from Edward's fingers, landing on the floor with a whisper that seemed to echo through the empty room. He stared at it, unable to reconcile the warmth of the Clara he knew with the icy dismissal on the page before him.

As the clock in the hall chimed the hour, Edward heard his father's laboured breathing from the study. He closed his eyes, feeling the loss and worry settle on his shoulders.

Edward's world seemed to shrink with each passing day. The vicarage, once a haven of warmth and laughter, now echoed with the sound of his father's wracking coughs. Reverend Thornton's illness cast a pall over every room, transforming the cheerful home into a place of hushed whispers and worried glances.

As his father's strength waned, Edward found himself shouldering more of the parish duties. He rose early to prepare sermons, his fingers ink-stained as he pored over his father's well-worn Bible.

"Edward, my boy," Reverend Thornton called weakly one morning. "I'm afraid I won't make it to Mrs Holloway's today. Her husband's passing... she needs comfort."

Edward nodded, swallowing the lump in his throat. "Of course, Father. I'll go."

He spent the afternoon with the grieving widow, offering what solace he could. As he walked home, the church bells rang out, signaling the start of choir practice. Edward's steps faltered, his heart aching at the sound. He could almost hear Clara's voice soaring above the rest, clear and pure as a mountain stream.

But those days were gone. Edward turned away from the church, quickening his pace back to the vicarage. His father needed him.

Weeks blurred into months. Edward's hands, once so nimble on the piano keys, now grew calloused from tending the garden and making minor repairs around the house. He missed the feeling of sheet music beneath his fingers, the swell of voices raised in harmony. But every time he thought of sitting down at the piano, his father would call out, needing help to move from his bed to his chair, or requiring another dose of medicine.

The parishioners noticed the change in their young Master Thornton. Gone was the bright-eyed youth who had led the choir with such passion. In his place stood a man with shadows under his eyes and a furrow etched permanently between his brows.

EDWARD'S PLIGHT

*E*dward's heart sank as he listened to the doctor's somber diagnosis. The words seemed to echo in the small study, each syllable hammering home the gravity of his father's condition.

"Extended rest and care, I'm afraid," Dr Horley said, his weathered face etched with concern. "Your father's lungs are weak. Any exertion could worsen his state."

Edward nodded, his throat tight. "And the cost of treatment?"

Dr Horley hesitated, then named a figure that made Edward's stomach lurch. It was more than their modest savings could bear.

As the doctor packed away his instruments, Edward's mind raced. The vicarage needed repairs, the roof leaked, and now there were medicines to buy. He glanced at his father, asleep in the armchair by the fire, looking smaller and more fragile than Edward had ever seen him.

That night, Edward sat at the kitchen table, surrounded by bills and ledgers. The numbers swam before his eyes, a relentless tide of red ink. He pushed aside the sheet music he'd been working on, a half-finished hymn now forgotten.

His gaze fell on the piano in the corner, shrouded in shadows. The keys, once a source of joy and inspiration, now seemed to mock him with their silence. Edward's fingers twitched, remembering the feel of the cool ivory beneath them. But the memory was quickly replaced by the sound of his father's laboured breathing from the next room.

With a heavy sigh, Edward reached for the local newspaper. He turned to the employment section, scanning the listings with growing desperation. His eyes landed on an advertisement for a clerk position at Hardcastle & Associates Counting House, a reputable accounting firm in town.

Edward's heart clenched. It wasn't the future he'd imagined for himself, but what choice did he have? The parish needed tending, his father needed care, and bills needed paying. His dreams of composing grand oratorios and leading choirs would have to wait.

∼

Edward stepped into the narrow, three-story building of Hardcastle & Associates Counting House, his heart heavy as the door closed behind him. The bustling commercial district outside faded away, replaced by the musty smell of old ledgers and ink.

Mr Hardcastle, a portly man with thinning hair, led Edward to his assigned desk. "You'll start with these accounts," he said, dropping a stack of papers onto the high wooden surface. "Mind your figures, Thornton. Accuracy is everything here."

Edward nodded, his fingers itching for piano keys as he picked up a quill. The scratching of nibs on paper filled the air, a far cry from the harmonious melodies he once created.

Days blurred into weeks. Edward's world shrank to columns

of numbers and endless calculations. He worked diligently, his natural attention to detail serving him well in this new role. But each evening, as he trudged home to care for his ailing father, his unfulfilled dreams pressed heavily upon him.

In quiet moments, Edward would catch himself humming softly, only to be startled by the harsh reality of his surroundings. The lively tunes that once danced in his mind grew fainter, replaced by the dull thud of ledger books and the rustle of papers.

Mr Hardcastle praised Edward's work, noting his accuracy and efficiency. Yet, these words of commendation rang hollow in Edward's ears. He longed for the soaring notes of a choir, the feel of organ keys beneath his fingers. Instead, he found himself trapped in a world of debits and credits, his passion for music fading like a distant echo.

A PRIVATE CONCERT

*E*ach tick of the grandfather clock in the corner was a reminder of the years that had slipped away within these gilded walls.

Clara caught a glimpse of her reflection in the gleaming surface of a serving tray. Despite the years of hard labour, her face remained youthful. Clara quickly looked away, uncomfortable with the stark contrast between her appearance and the weariness that settled deep in her bones.

As she worked, Clara felt Mrs Flint's gaze boring into her back. She turned, meeting the older woman's eyes for a brief moment before Mrs Flint looked away, her lips pursed in a thin line of disapproval.

The tension in the house had been building for weeks, an unspoken current that set everyone on edge. Clara noticed the way the other servants whispered when she entered a room, their conversations dying away as if they'd been discussing some great secret.

Even Mr Phineas, usually so proper and aloof, seemed to regard her with a mix of pity and concern. Clara couldn't shake the feeling that something was about to change, that the delicate balance of her life at Flint Manor was teetering on the edge of upheaval.

As she moved to polish the next piece of silverware, Clara's fingers trembled slightly. She took a deep breath, steadying herself. Whatever was coming, she would face it with the same quiet determination that had carried her through these past years.

Later that same day, Clara felt Mrs Flint's eyes on her yet again as she dusted the ornate mantelpiece in the drawing room. That gaze pressed down on her shoulders, making each movement feel like a struggle against an invisible force.

"Miss Winters," Mrs Flint's said sharply. "You've missed a spot. Again."

Clara turned, her heart sinking. "I'm sorry, ma'am. I'll rectify it immediately."

Mrs Flint scoffed. "See that you do. Your incompetence is becoming quite tiresome."

The words stung, but Clara kept her face impassive. She'd learned long ago that showing any reaction only invited further criticism.

The words echoed in Clara's mind long after Mrs Flint had swept from the room. She stood there, dust cloth clutched tightly in her hand, fighting back the tears that threatened to fall.

The urge to sing, to let her voice soar and carry away her troubles, was almost overwhelming. But Clara pressed her lips together, trapping the melody inside. She wouldn't give Mrs Flint the satisfaction of catching her again.

Instead, Clara channeled her frustration into her work, attacking the dust with renewed vigour. Each stroke of the cloth became an act of defiance, a silent rebellion against the constraints placed upon her.

As she worked, Clara allowed the music to play in her mind, a private concert that no one could take from her. It wasn't the same as singing aloud, but it was something. A small flame of hope that refused to be extinguished, no matter how hard Mrs Flint tried to snuff it out.

A PAINFUL PAST

Clara's mind drifted as she polished. The house stood silent, most of its inhabitants retired for the evening. In this rare moment of solitude, a melody bubbled up from deep within her, and before she could stop herself, she began to hum.

The tune was soft, barely audible even in the quiet hallway, but to Clara it felt like a balm on her weary soul. She let herself get lost in the gentle rise and fall of the notes.

"You!"

The harsh voice shattered the peace, and Clara's eyes flew open. Mrs Flint stood at the end of the hall, her face contorted with fury.

"I thought I made myself clear about your infernal caterwauling!"

Clara's heart pounded as Mrs Flint advanced, backing her into a corner. "I'm sorry, ma'am. I didn't think anyone would hear—"

"Didn't think? Of course you didn't think!" Mrs Flint's words dripped with venom. "You're just like all the rest, flaunting your voice, believing you're destined for greatness."

Clara shrank back, but there was nowhere to go. Mrs Flint loomed over her, trembling with barely contained rage.

"You want to know something, Miss Winters? I was like you once. Young, foolish, thinking my voice would carry me to the heights of society." Mrs Flint's laugh was bitter and sharp. "I had dreams of packed concert halls, of thunderous applause."

Her voice dropped to a whisper, thick with emotion. "But do you know what I discovered? My voice was mediocre at best. Oh, it was pleasant enough in small gatherings, but on stage?" She shook her head. "It was pitiful. And my singing teacher made sure to remind me of that fact every lesson."

Clara stood frozen, scarcely daring to breathe as Mrs Flint continued.

"And then came the night of my debut. The moment I'd dreamed of for years. And my last chance to prove to everyone, who doubted me, wrong!" Mrs Flint's eyes took on a faraway look. "I stepped out onto that stage, and do you know what happened?"

She didn't wait for Clara to respond. "I froze. The words wouldn't come. My throat closed up, and all I could do was stand there, gaping like a fish while the audience tittered."

Mrs Flint's gaze snapped back to Clara, her eyes burning with a mixture of pain and anger. "That was the end of my dreams. She refused to teach me after that... One moment of weakness, and everything I'd worked for crumbled to dust."

Clara stood frozen, her heart pounding as Mrs Flint's words hung heavy in the air between them. The older woman's face twisted with a kaleidoscope of emotions – pain, anger, and something deeper that Clara couldn't quite name. In that moment, she saw Mrs Flint not as the stern mistress of the house, but as a woman haunted by the ghosts of her own shattered dreams.

Mrs Flint's eyes bore into Clara, searching for something – understanding, perhaps, or the mockery she seemed to expect.

Clara opened her mouth to speak, but no words came. What could she possibly say in the face of such raw pain?

Her silence stretched on, and Clara watched as something shifted in Mrs Flint's gaze. The vulnerability that had briefly softened her features hardened once more, replaced by a familiar hostility. But now there was something else there too – a burning jealousy that made Clara's skin prickle with unease.

"You think you're better than me, don't you?" Mrs Flint hissed. "With your angelic voice and your youth. You probably pity poor, bitter Mrs Flint."

Clara shook her head frantically, desperate to dispel the notion. "No, ma'am, I—"

"Don't lie to me!" Mrs Flint's voice rose sharply, making Clara flinch. "I see the way you look at me, the way you all look at me. You think I'm some dried-up old crone who never amounted to anything."

The venom in Mrs Flint's words stung, but beneath it, Clara could hear the pain of old wounds ripped open anew. She wanted to reach out, to offer some words of comfort, but Mrs Flint's eyes flashed with a warning that kept her rooted to the spot.

"Well, let me tell you something, Miss Winters," Mrs Flint continued, her voice dropping to a venomous whisper. "Your voice won't save you. Talent isn't enough. The world out there will chew you up and spit you out, just like it did to me."

Clara wanted to protest, to defend herself, but the raw pain in the older woman's eyes silenced her. The hallway suddenly felt suffocating, the polishing cloth forgotten in Clara's trembling hand.

Mrs Flint's face twisted into a cruel smile. "You think your voice is a gift? It's a curse. It will lead you down a path of disappointment and heartbreak. Just like it did to me."

Clara swallowed hard, fighting back tears. She thought of all the times her voice had brought her comfort, had connected her to memories of her parents and happier days. How could something that felt so right be wrong?

"I..." Clara's voice quavered. She steadied herself. "I'm sorry for what happened to you, Mrs Flint. Truly, I am. But my voice... it's part of who I am. I can't just—"

"Silence!" Mrs Flint's hand shot out, gripping Clara's arm with surprising strength. "You will learn your place in this house, girl. No more singing, no more humming, no more of your infernal noise. Do you understand me?"

Clara nodded mutely, her arm aching where Mrs Flint's fingers dug into her flesh.

"Good," Mrs Flint released her grip, smoothing her skirts as if nothing had happened. "Now, finish your work and get out of my sight. And remember, Miss Winters, I'm watching you. Always watching."

With that, Mrs Flint turned on her heel and stalked away, leaving Clara alone in the hallway. Clara's legs gave way, and she sank to the floor, her back pressed against the wall. She drew her knees to her chest, burying her face in her arms as silent sobs wracked her body.

Mrs Flint's words pressed down on her, threatening to crush the last remnants of hope she'd been clinging to. Clara had always believed her voice was a gift, a connection to something greater than herself. Now, that belief lay shattered at her feet, leaving her feeling more alone than ever before.

ANCHORS IN THE STORM

Clara's days at Flint Manor became a blur of endless toil and exhaustion. Each morning, she rose before dawn, her body aching from the previous day's labours. The list of tasks seemed to grow longer with each passing week, as Mrs Flint found new and increasingly arduous chores for her to complete.

She scrubbed floors until her hands were raw, polished silver until her arms trembled, and hauled heavy buckets of water up and down the stairs until her legs felt like lead. The work was relentless, leaving Clara physically drained and emotionally spent.

Miss Crabtree's sharp eyes followed Clara's every move, quick to point out any perceived flaw in her work. Mr Phineas, too, seemed to have taken a renewed interest in scrutinising Clara's performance. Their constant vigilance turned even the simplest tasks into tests of endurance.

"You missed a spot there, girl," Miss Crabtree's voice cut through the air as Clara polished the banister for the third time that morning. "Do it again, and properly this time."

Clara bit her lip, fighting back tears of frustration as she retraced her steps. No matter how hard she tried, it never seemed to be enough.

Yet, even in the midst of this gruelling existence, Clara found small moments of respite. Betsy and Mary, her fellow housemaids, became silent allies in her struggle. During shared chores, they would whisper words of encouragement, their presence a balm to Clara's weary spirit.

One evening, as Clara dragged herself to the kitchen for her meagre supper, she found a small bundle tucked behind a flour sack. Inside was a thick slice of fresh bread and a pat of butter – a luxury she hadn't tasted in weeks. She knew it could only have come from Cook, and the simple act of kindness brought tears to her eyes.

During her increasingly rare moments of respite, Clara would seek Old John out in the gardens. His weathered face would crinkle with concern as he took in her exhausted state.

"Remember, lass," he'd say, his voice low and soothing, "even the harshest winter can't stop the flowers from blooming come spring. You've got that same strength in you."

Clara's spirit, once vibrant and full of song, had been battered by the relentless demands of life at Flint Manor. Yet, as the days turned into weeks, something within her began to shift. The crushing weight of Mrs Flint's cruelty no longer seemed to penetrate as deeply as it once had.

Each morning, as Clara rose from her narrow bed, she took a moment to breathe deeply and steel herself for the day ahead. She moved through her tasks with a newfound focus, her movements efficient and purposeful. The harsh words that once stung now seemed to glance off her, like raindrops on a windowpane.

"You call this clean?" Mrs Flint's voice dripped with disdain as she ran a gloved finger along the mantel. "I've seen pigs with better hygiene."

Clara met Mrs Flint's gaze steadily. "I'll do it again, ma'am," she said, her voice calm and even. She reached for her cleaning cloth, noting with quiet satisfaction the flicker of surprise in Mrs Flint's eyes.

As she re-polished the mantel, Clara hummed softly to herself, the melody barely audible. It was a small act of defiance, but it fuelled the ember of hope that still burned within her. She would not let this place extinguish her love for music, no matter how hard they tried.

In the kitchen, Clara worked alongside Betsy and Mary, their shared glances speaking volumes. They had noticed the change in her, the way she carried herself with a quiet dignity that seemed to grow stronger with each passing day.

"You're different lately," Betsy whispered as they peeled potatoes side by side. "It's like... like you've found some hidden strength."

Clara offered a small smile. "Perhaps I have," she murmured. "Or perhaps I'm just learning to weather the storm."

CLARA STOOD before Mrs Flint in the dimly lit study, her hands clasped tightly behind her back. The older woman's eyes glittered with malice as she circled Clara like a predator stalking its prey. Clara's heart raced, but she kept her expression neutral, refusing to give Mrs Flint the satisfaction of seeing her fear.

"It seems," Mrs Flint began, her voice dripping with disdain, "that you still haven't learned your place in this household, girl." She stopped directly in front of Clara, her face inches away. "Your continued... resistance... is most displeasing."

Clara fought the urge to step back, instead meeting Mrs Flint's gaze steadily. "I've completed all tasks assigned to me, ma'am," she said, her voice quiet but firm.

"Oh, you've done the work, yes. But your spirit..." Mrs Flint reached out, grasping Clara's chin roughly. "Your spirit remains unbroken. And that, my dear, simply won't do."

Clara felt a tear form at the corner of her eyes as Mrs Flint's grip tightened. The woman's next words sent a chill down her spine.

"Let me make myself perfectly clear," Mrs Flint hissed. "If you do not learn to comply fully with the demands of this household – if I see even a hint of defiance or hear so much as a whispered note – I will make certain you are sent somewhere far worse than this. Perhaps a workhouse, where that pretty voice of yours will be drowned out by the clanging of machines and the cries of the truly wretched."

Mrs Flint released Clara's chin, pushing her away slightly. "Do I make myself clear?"

For a moment, Clara felt her resolve waver. The threat of an even harsher fate loomed before her, dark and terrifying. But then, unbidden, a memory surfaced – Edward's warm brown eyes, filled with determination as he promised to believe in her always.

Clara straightened her spine. She met Mrs Flint's gaze once more, her blue eyes clear and unwavering. "Yes, ma'am," she said, her voice steady. "I understand."

As Mrs Flint dismissed her with a wave of her hand, Clara turned to leave the study. Her steps were measured and calm, betraying none of the turmoil within. She may have agreed to Mrs Flint's terms outwardly, but inwardly, Clara's resolve had only hardened.

She would endure. She would persist. No matter what came her way, Clara would find the strength to weather it. The music in her heart, the memories of Edward and the promises they'd made – these would be her anchors in the storms to come.

INTO THE COLD

Clara stirred in her narrow bed, the cold air nipping at her nose as she reluctantly opened her eyes. The room was still dark, but a faint glow from the snow-covered grounds outside filtered through the small window. She sat up, shivering as the threadbare blanket fell away from her shoulders.

Christmas Eve. The thought brought a mixture of emotions – a faint echo of joy from happier times, quickly overshadowed by the reality of her current situation. Clara knew that for her, today would be no different from any other day at Flint Manor.

She dressed quickly, her fingers clumsy with cold as she buttoned her worn dress. Clara paused at the small mirror propped on her dresser, running a hand through her auburn hair before twisting it into a neat bun.

As she made her way down the narrow servant's staircase, Clara could hear the distant sounds of the household stirring. The rich aroma of fresh bread wafted up from the kitchen, mingling with the scent of pine from the Christmas decorations that adorned the main parts of the house.

Clara entered the kitchen, grateful for the warmth from the large stove. Cook nodded a greeting, who knew what time she had woken up, her hands busy kneading dough for the day's bread. "Mornin', Clara," she said softly. "Best get started on the grates in the drawing room. Mrs Flint wants everything spotless as usual."

With a quiet sigh, Clara gathered her cleaning supplies. As she made her way to the drawing room, she caught glimpses of the elaborate decorations through partially open doors – garlands of evergreen, red ribbons, and glittering ornaments. The difference between the festive cheer in the main rooms and the austere conditions of the servants' quarters was not lost on her.

In the drawing room, Clara knelt before the fireplace, her back already aching as she began to scrub the grate. Outside, snow continued to fall, blanketing the world in white. Despite the beauty of the scene, Clara felt a heaviness in her heart. This was not how she had imagined spending Christmas Eve, all those years ago when she still had hope for a brighter future.

Clara's hands were raw and aching from scrubbing the grate when she heard Mrs Flint's sharp voice calling her name. With a sinking feeling in her stomach, Clara rose to her feet, brushing soot from her apron as she made her way to the parlour.

The warmth from the crackling fire hit Clara like a wall as she entered, making her shiver involuntarily. Mrs Flint sat primly on a plush armchair, her pale eyes narrowed as they fixed on Clara.

"There you are," Mrs Flint said, her tone dripping with disdain. "I have an urgent task for you."

Clara stood silently, waiting for the inevitable blow to fall.

"We're in desperate need of supplies for tonight's dinner," Mrs Flint continued, a cruel smile playing at the corners of her mouth. "You're to go to the market at once and fetch everything on this list."

She thrust a piece of paper into Clara's hands. Clara's heart sank as she saw the extensive list of items, knowing full well that most of these were already stocked in the manor's pantry.

"But Mrs Flint," Clara began hesitantly, "it's quite a distance to the market, and in this weather—"

"Are you questioning my orders?" Mrs Flint's voice cut through the air like a whip. "You'll walk there and back, of course. We can't spare the carriage for a mere servant's errand."

Clara's shoulders slumped in defeat. "Yes, Mrs Flint," she murmured.

"And make sure you're back in time to help with the dinner preparations," Mrs Flint added, turning back to the fire. "Now go."

Clara left the warm parlour, the list clutched in her trembling hand. As she retrieved her thin coat from the servant's hall, she could hear the wind howling outside, promising a long and miserable journey ahead.

The wind immediately whipped at her thin coat as she stepped out into the biting cold. She clutched the list tightly in her gloved hand, her breath forming small clouds in the frosty air. The snow crunched beneath her worn boots as she made her way down the long driveway of Flint Manor.

As she reached the iron gates, Clara paused, looking back at the imposing structure. Through one of the windows, she caught a glimpse of Mrs Flint's smug face watching her departure. Clara's jaw clenched, but she forced herself to turn away and push forward.

The road stretched out before her, a white ribbon disappearing into the distance. Clara tucked her chin into her collar, trying to shield her face from the relentless wind. Each step was a struggle against the elements, her legs already aching from the effort of trudging through the deep snow.

As she walked, Clara's mind wandered to the kitchen she had left behind. She could almost smell Cook's fresh bread, could almost feel the heat from the stove. The contrast with her current situation was stark, and Clara felt a lump form in her throat.

Back at the manor, Betsy and Mary watched Clara's retreating figure from a window in the servant's hall. Betsy's brow furrowed with concern. "It's not right, sending her out in this weather," she murmured.

Mary nodded, her usual bravado subdued. "She'll catch her death out there, she will."

The two housemaids exchanged worried glances, both knowing there was nothing they could do to help their friend. The tyranny of Mrs Flint's rule over the household was absolute, and they could only hope that Clara would return safely.

A GRUELLING TASK

Clara trudged through the snow, her worn boots sinking into the deep drifts with each step. The wind howled around her, whipping her thin coat and stinging her exposed skin.

As she walked, Clara's mind drifted to warmer times. She thought of Edward, his kind eyes and gentle smile. The memory of their shared hymns echoed in her mind, a welcome contrast to the harsh winter surrounding her. For a brief moment, she felt a flicker of warmth, but it quickly faded as another gust of icy wind cut through her.

The hours dragged on, each step more difficult than the last. Clara's entire body ached from the cold, her limbs growing stiff and unresponsive. She pushed forward, knowing that stopping would only make things worse. The need to complete her errand and return to the relative safety of the manor drove her onward.

Clara's breath came in ragged gasps, forming small clouds in the frigid air. She paused for a moment, leaning against a snow-covered tree to catch her breath. Her eyes scanned the white landscape, searching desperately for any sign of the town. The endless expanse of snow stretched out before her, broken only by the occasional dark shape of a tree or fence post.

∼

Clara stumbled into the market square, her legs trembling from exhaustion. The cheerful bustle of townsfolk and vendors felt almost surreal after her arduous journey through the silent, snow-covered countryside. Colourful garlands and wreaths adorned the stalls, their festive cheer a stark contrast to Clara's weary state.

She blinked, momentarily disoriented by the sudden shift from isolation to the lively crowd. The scent of roasted chestnuts and mulled wine wafted through the air, mingling with the winter breeze. Clara's stomach growled, reminding her that she hadn't eaten since her small breakfast at dawn.

Shaking off her fatigue, Clara focused on her task. She weaved through the throng of last-minute shoppers, her eyes scanning the stalls for the items on Mrs Flint's list.

As Clara moved from stall to stall, she felt curious glances upon her, their expressions of sympathy and poorly concealed interest. She heard whispers as she passed, catching fragments of gossip.

"Poor dear, out in this weather..."

"...working on Christmas Eve, of all days..."

Clara kept her head down, her cheeks flushing with a combination of embarrassment and the biting cold. She quickened her pace, eager to complete her task and escape the pitying stares.

With each purchase, the burden in her arms grew heavier. Clara's muscles ached from the long walk and the added weight of the supplies. She struggled to maintain her balance on the slippery cobblestones, her worn boots offering little traction.

Clara's arms trembled under the weight of the packages as

she trudged through the snow-covered streets. The cold gnawed at her cheeks, turning them a raw, angry red. Her fingers, numb and aching, struggled to maintain their grip on the parcels.

She focused on the rhythmic crunch of snow beneath her feet, desperate to block out the bone-deep chill that had settled into her body. Each step felt like a monumental effort, her legs leaden with exhaustion.

The cheerful glow of lights in shop windows mocked her misery. Clara averted her gaze, fixing her eyes on the path ahead. She couldn't afford to be distracted by thoughts of warmth and comfort, not when she still had so far to go.

A gust of wind whipped around her, tugging at her, threatening to topple her precarious balance. Clara stumbled, her heart leaping into her throat as she fought to stay upright. The packages shifted dangerously in her arms.

Gritting her teeth, Clara righted herself and pressed on. She focused on the simple act of moving forward – left foot, right foot, left foot again. The world narrowed to this singular task, everything else fading into the background.

As she rounded a corner, the wind intensified, driving icy pellets of snow into her face. Clara ducked her head, using her body to shield the packages from the worst of the onslaught. She couldn't risk damaging Mrs Flint's precious supplies, no matter how much her body protested.

The streets began to empty as the weather worsened, leaving Clara alone with the howling wind and her own laboured breathing. She pushed herself onward, each step a small victory against the elements and her own exhaustion.

SOLACE IN MUSIC

Clara paused in her arduous journey, her breath catching as she found herself face-to-face with St. Paul's Church. The familiar stone facade loomed before her, a beacon of warmth and memories amidst the swirling snow. She blinked, realising she must have passed it earlier without noticing, her mind too focused on the task at hand.

The church stood adorned with festive decorations, evergreen garlands draped gracefully along its walls and a large wreath hanging proudly on the heavy wooden doors. Soft light spilled from the windows, casting a golden glow on the snow-covered steps. The sight stirred something deep within Clara, a bittersweet ache that threatened to overwhelm her.

For a moment, she allowed herself to remember. The countless Sundays spent here, her voice soaring with the choir, the pride in Reverend Thornton's eyes as she sang. The companionship of Edward, their shared love of music echoing through these very halls. It all felt like a lifetime ago, yet the memories were as fresh as the snow beneath her feet.

The warm light beckoned to her, promising respite from the biting cold and the gruelling journey ahead. She longed to

THE ORPHAN'S CHRISTMAS HYMN

step inside, to feel the embrace of familiar hymns and the comfort of faith that had sustained her through so many hardships.

Clara's feet carried her closer to the church, drawn by an invisible force. The iron fence pressed cold against her body as she leaned against it, her breath forming small clouds in the frigid air. Through the frost-covered window, she caught sight of Edward, his tall figure moving purposefully as he arranged chairs for the choir.

Her heart constricted at the sight of him. He looked older, more serious, the boyish charm she remembered replaced by a man's determination. Clara's mind flooded with memories – their shared laughter, the music they'd created together, the promises they'd made. But those promises had withered like leaves in winter, carried away by unanswered letters and long years of silence.

Clara shivered. She knew she should move on, continue her arduous journey back to Flint Manor. Mrs Flint would be furious if she delayed. Yet something kept her rooted to the spot, her eyes fixed on the warmth and life within the church.

Almost without realising it, Clara began to sing. Her voice, soft and hesitant at first, grew stronger as the familiar hymn flowed from her lips. The melody drifted on the wind, a quiet defiance against the bitter cold.

"Silent night, holy night
All is calm, all is bright
Round yon Virgin, Mother and Child
Holy infant so tender and mild
Sleep in heavenly peace

Sleep in heavenly peace"

As she sang, Clara felt a contentment bloom within her, pushing back against the chill that had settled in her bones. For a moment, she wasn't a lowly maid weighed down by parcels and Mrs Flint's demands. She was Clara Winters, the girl with the voice of an angel, finding solace in the music that had always been her refuge.

A FAMILIAR VOICE

*E*dward was surrounded by the bustle of last-minute preparations for the Christmas Eve service. The scent of pine and beeswax filled the air as parishioners hung garlands and arranged candles. Edward's hands trembled slightly as he sorted through sheet music, his mind a whirlwind of conflicting emotions.

"Mr Thornton, where should we place these poinsettias?" Mrs Higgins, a rosy-cheeked woman, called out.

Edward looked up, forcing a smile. "Near the altar, please. They'll frame the nativity scene nicely."

As he watched Mrs Higgins move away with the potted plants, Edward's gaze drifted to the empty choir stalls. The absence of Mr Hawthorne, the choirmaster, weighed heavily on him. The man's sudden illness had left a void that Edward reluctantly stepped in to fill.

He ran his fingers over the worn pages of the hymnal, memories of countless hours spent practicing flooding back. The familiar melodies seemed to whisper in his ear, urging him to take his place at the organ. But responsibility pulled him in another direction.

Edward's father was still growing weaker by the day. The cost of his treatments forcing Edward to work even more hours at the counting house. The ledgers and figures that now filled his days were a far cry from the harmonies that once consumed his thoughts.

"Edward, my boy, how are the preparations coming along?" Reverend Thornton's voice, weaker than it once was but still warm, broke through Edward's reverie.

Edward turned to see his father leaning heavily on his cane, a pallor to his skin that made Edward's heart clench. "Everything's nearly ready, Father. You should be resting."

The reverend waved off his son's concern. "I couldn't miss this. It does my heart good to see you back where you belong."

Edward swallowed hard, torn between the joy of his father's pride and the guilt of his own divided loyalties. He opened his mouth to respond, but the words caught in his throat as a hauntingly familiar voice drifted through the church doors.

The pure, crystalline tones of *Silent Night* filled the air, each note resonating deep within his soul. For a moment, he stood frozen, his mind reeling as memories flooded back – memories of a young girl with auburn hair and sapphire eyes, her voice lifting above the choir in perfect harmony.

"Clara," he whispered, the name catching in his throat.

Without a second thought, Edward dropped the sheet music he'd been holding, papers scattering across the floor. He barely registered the concerned calls of his father and the parishioners as he bolted towards the nearest window.

His fingers, clumsy with urgency, fumbled with the latch. Finally, he wrenched the window open, a blast of frigid air rushing in. Edward leaned out, his eyes frantically scanning the snow-covered street below. The falling snow blurred his vision, and he wiped at his eyes with his sleeve, desperate for a clearer view.

"Where are you?" he murmured, his breath forming small clouds in the icy air.

"Edward!" His father's voice, tinged with worry, barely registered. "What on earth are you doing, boy?"

Edward's heart raced as he turned away from the window, his mind reeling with the possibility that Clara was so near. He couldn't waste a moment trying to explain the situation to his father or the confused parishioners. Every second that ticked by was another chance for Clara to slip away, to vanish into the snowy streets like a ghost from his past.

"I'll be right back," he called over his shoulder, already striding towards the church doors, grabbing his coat on the way.

COMING HOME

Clara's voice caught in her throat as she locked eyes with Edward. The familiar warmth of his gaze melted away the biting cold that had numbed her fingers and toes. For a heartbeat, she forgot about the heavy packages in her arms, the long trek back to Flint Manor, and the years of silence between them.

Edward took a hesitant step forward, his boots crunching in the fresh snow. "Clara?" he breathed.

She wanted to run to him, to throw her arms around him and never let go. But the weight of unanswered letters and broken promises held her back. Clara swallowed hard, her throat tight with unshed tears.

"Edward," she managed, her voice hoarse from singing and the cold. "I..."

He closed the distance between them, his eyes never leaving her face. "I heard you singing. I thought I was imagining things, but... it's really you."

Clara shifted the packages in her arms, suddenly aware of how bedraggled she must look. Her cheeks flushed with a mixture of cold and embarrassment. "I was just passing by. I have to get back to—"

Clara felt Edward's warm hands on her arms, steadying her as she trembled from both cold and emotion. His touch sent a jolt through her, awakening feelings she'd long buried beneath her daily struggles at Flint Manor.

"You're freezing," Edward said, his brow furrowed with concern. "Please, come inside. Just for a moment."

Clara hesitated, her mind racing. She knew she should refuse, that Mrs Flint would be furious. But the earnestness in Edward's eyes weakened her resolve. She found herself nodding, unable to form words.

Edward guided her gently into the church, his hand at the small of her back. The heat of the building enveloped Clara like a comforting embrace, thawing her frozen limbs. She blinked, adjusting to the soft glow of candlelight after the harsh glare of snow.

Whispers rippled through the gathered parishioners and choir members. Clara caught snippets of hushed conversations, her name repeated with a mixture of surprise and curiosity. She clutched her market parcels tighter, suddenly aware of how out of place she must look in her threadbare coat and work-worn hands.

Edward led her to a bench near the choir loft, his movements quick but tender. "Here," he said, shrugging off his own coat and draping it around her shoulders. The weight of it, still warm from his body, made Clara's eyes prick with tears.

"Edward, I can't—" she began, but he silenced her with a gentle shake of his head.

"You're shivering," he insisted, his hands lingering on her shoulders. "Please, just for a moment."

Clara nodded, allowing herself to sink into his coat and the familiar scent that clung to it. She set her parcels beside her on the bench, flexing her stiff fingers.

"I'm so sorry," Clara murmured, her voice barely above a whisper. "I didn't mean to interrupt. You must be terribly busy with the Christmas Eve service, and here I am, barging in and causing a fuss."

Clara's gaze dropped to her lap, where her work-worn hands twisted nervously in the folds of Edward's coat. She was acutely aware of the whispers that still rippled through the church, the curious glances from parishioners who no doubt remembered her from years past.

"I shouldn't have come in," she continued, the words tumbling out in a rush. "It was foolish of me to think... I mean, after all this time..."

Edward's hand gently tilted her chin up, forcing her to meet his gaze once more. His touch sent a shiver through her that had nothing to do with the cold.

"Clara," he said, his voice soft but firm. "You have nothing to apologize for."

He shook his head, a smile spreading across his face that reached all the way to his eyes. It was the same smile she remembered from their days at St Mary's, the one that had always made her feel as if everything would be alright.

"Seeing you again," Edward continued, "hearing your voice after all this time... it's not an interruption. It's a gift."

Clara felt her breath catch in her throat at the sincerity in his words. The joy and relief that radiated from Edward was palpable, washing away years of doubt and loneliness in an instant.

Her heart skipped a beat as Edward's expression suddenly turned serious. His brow furrowed, and he leaned in closer, his voice lowered.

"Clara, I... I have to ask. That letter you sent, telling me you were happier without me, that you didn't want to hear from me anymore... Did you really mean it?"

Clara's eyes widened in shock, her mouth falling open. She

shook her head slowly, bewilderment etched across her features. "Edward, I... I never sent such a letter. Never!"

"I wrote to you so many times," she continued, her voice trembling. "I poured my heart out in those letters, asking after you, wondering why you'd gone silent. But I never received a reply. Not one."

Edward's face mirrored her astonishment. He took a step back, running a hand through his hair in disbelief. "But I wrote to you, Clara. Countless times. I thought... I thought you'd moved on, found a better life at the Flint estate."

Clara shook her head vehemently, tears pricking at the corners of her eyes. "No, Edward. My life there has been... It's been far from what I'd hoped. I've missed you terribly. I've missed our music, our friendship. I would never have dismissed you from my life."

As the truth of their situation dawned on them both, a heavy silence fell between them. Clara's mind raced, trying to make sense of this revelation. How could their letters have gone astray? Who could have intercepted them?

Edward's eyes met hers, filled with a mixture of relief and lingering confusion. Clara saw her own feelings reflected in his gaze – the pain of perceived rejection, the years of loneliness, and now, a spark of hope rekindling between them.

"Mrs Flint," Clara said, her voice filled with a certainty that surprised even her. "It must have been her. She intercepted our letters, Edward. And she..." Clara's voice caught as the full weight of the deception hit her. "She must have forged that letter to you."

Edward's eyes widened, then narrowed with a determination Clara hadn't seen since their days at St Mary's. He clenched his fists at his sides, his knuckles turning white.

"How dare she," he growled. "To meddle in our lives like that, to cause us both so much pain..."

Clara reached out, placing a hand on Edward's arm. The

touch seemed to ground him, and he took a deep breath, his shoulders relaxing slightly.

"We won't let her separate us again," Edward declared, his voice firm and resolute. "Not now that we know the truth."

Clara nodded, feeling a spark of defiance ignite within her. For so long, she had felt powerless, trapped in a life she never wanted. But now, with Edward by her side once more, she felt a strength she had almost forgotten.

"No," Clara agreed, her voice growing stronger. "We won't let her, or anyone else, come between us again."

Clara's heart swelled with emotion as she gazed into Edward's eyes, tears glistening in her own.

"Oh, Edward," she whispered. "I've never forgotten you. Not for a single day."

She clasped her hands together, pressing them to her chest as if to contain the flood of feelings threatening to overwhelm her. "There were so many nights," Clara's words tumbled out in a rush, "when I'd lie awake in that tiny attic room, thinking of you. Of us. Of the music we made together.

"I'd hum our songs under my breath, trying to remember every note, every harmony. It was the only thing that kept me going some days."

She looked up at him again, a watery smile breaking through her tears. "I dreamed of the day we'd sing together again, of the future we once talked about. Those dreams... they were my refuge, Edward. My solace in the darkest times."

Edward reached out, gently taking Clara's hands in his own. His thumbs traced small circles on the backs of her hands, a soothing gesture that sent a shiver down Clara's spine. "Every time I sat at the piano," Edward said, "every time I heard a hymn or caught a strain of music on the street, I thought of you."

Clara listened intently as Edward's expression grew somber. His shoulders sagged slightly.

"Clara, there's so much I need to tell you. My father... he fell ill not long after you left. It was sudden and severe."

Clara's heart clenched at the news. She remembered Reverend Thornton's kindness, how he had championed her singing and given her hope during her darkest days at St Mary's, but also how he had looked at her with such surprise and sorrow, believing Mrs Blackthorn's words.

Edward continued, his eyes distant as if reliving the memory. "The treatments were expensive, and the vicarage needed repairs. I couldn't... I couldn't pursue my dreams of becoming a choirmaster. Not when my father needed me."

Clara squeezed his hand gently, encouraging him to go on. Edward met her gaze, a flicker of gratitude in his eyes.

"I took a position at Hardcastle & Associates Counting House," he said, his voice flat. "It's not what I wanted, but it pays the bills. The work is... well, it's dreary, to be honest. Endless columns of numbers, day in and day out."

Clara's heart ached for Edward. She knew all too well the pain of setting aside one's passion for duty. She thought of her own days filled with endless chores at Flint Manor, the music in her heart silenced by Mrs. Flint's cruel demands.

"But tonight," Edward continued, a spark returning to his eyes, "tonight is different. Our regular choirmaster fell ill, and they asked me to step in for the Christmas Eve service."

Clara felt a surge of joy at the news. "Oh, Edward, that's wonderful!"

He nodded, a genuine smile spreading across his face. "It is. For the first time in so long, I feel... alive again. The music, Clara. It's like coming home."

FORGIVENESS

Clara's heart skipped a beat as she saw Reverend Thornton approaching. His steps were slower than she remembered, his frame slightly stooped, but his eyes still held that same warmth and kindness she'd known years ago.

"Clara, my dear," Reverend Thornton said, his voice wavering. "It's so wonderful to see you again."

Clara felt Edward's hand squeeze hers gently as the Reverend continued, "I... I owe you a profound apology. The way I handled your situation all those years ago was... it was wrong. I should have fought harder for you, should have seen through Mrs Blackthorn's lies."

Clara's eyes welled with tears, but she managed a smile. "Reverend Thornton, please. You have no need to apologise. I forgave you long ago."

The old man's eyes glistened. "You're too kind, my dear. But I want you to know that I've worked tirelessly to make things right. Mrs Blackthorn... she's no longer at St Mary's."

Clara heart skipped a beat. She hadn't dared to hope for such news.

"They have a new headmistress now," Reverend Thornton

continued. "Miss Rose. She's a kind and righteous woman, Clara. The children... they're happy now. Cared for as they should be."

Clara felt a weight she hadn't even realised she'd been carrying lift from her shoulders. The thought of other children suffering as she had under Mrs Blackthorn's cruel reign had haunted her. But now...

"Thank you," Clara whispered, her voice thick with emotion. "Thank you for not giving up on them."

Reverend Thornton reached out, patting her hand gently. "It was the least I could do, my dear. And I want you to know that you'll always have a place here, Clara. Always."

Clara felt a sense of belonging she thought she'd lost forever. She looked from Reverend Thornton to Edward, then back to the church behind them. For the first time in years, she felt truly at home.

"Clara," Edward said, his voice soft but filled with excitement, "would you join us for the service tonight? We would love to have your voice in the choir."

For a moment, Clara couldn't breathe. The invitation hung in the air, a lifeline back to everything she'd lost – her music, her passion, her sense of belonging. She opened her mouth to accept without hesitation, but then her gaze fell on the packages lying beside her.

Mrs Flint's voice echoed in her mind, cold and cruel. Clara's shoulders slumped slightly as the reality of her situation crashed over her.

But as quickly as the doubt had come, it vanished. Clara looked at the packages again, really looked at them. She saw them for what they truly were – not a duty or an obligation, but a spiteful attempt to crush her spirit. Mrs Flint had sent her out into this bitter cold on Christmas Eve for no real reason, just to assert her power and keep Clara away from any joy the holiday might bring.

Clara straightened her spine, a spark of defiance igniting in her. She met Edward's gaze, seeing all the love and hope she'd been missing reflected there. Then she glanced at Reverend Thornton, his kind eyes full of understanding and encouragement.

"I..." Clara began, her voice growing stronger with each word, "I would be honoured to join the choir tonight."

MR FLINT'S TRANSFORMATION

Reginald Flint stepped out of the carriage, his polished shoes sinking into the fresh snow. The crisp winter air nipped at his cheeks. He turned, extending a gloved hand to assist his wife, Beatrice, as she descended.

Beatrice's face was pinched with irritation, her lips moving in a constant stream of complaints. Reginald had long since mastered the art of appearing attentive while letting her words wash over him like white noise.

"...and that ungrateful little wretch has the audacity to disappear on Christmas Eve of all days!" Beatrice huffed, adjusting her fur-trimmed coat.

Reginald grunted noncommittally, his eyes scanning the churchyard. St Paul's stood before them, its stone walls adorned with wreaths and garlands. The warm glow of candlelight spilled from the windows.

He nodded curtly to Mr Hardcastle, a business associate, who was ascending the steps with his family. The man's eldest son had recently joined Reginald's company as a clerk. What was the lad's name again? Charles? Richard? It hardly mattered.

"Reginald, are you even listening to me?" Beatrice's sharp tone cut through his musings.

"Of course, my dear," he replied smoothly, offering his arm. "Shall we?"

As they made their way towards the church entrance, Reginald acknowledged the respectful nods and murmured greetings from other parishioners. He was acutely aware of the eyes upon them, assessing their attire, their demeanour, their very presence on this occasion.

Beatrice's grip on his arm tightened as they passed Lady Havisham. The two women exchanged icy smiles, a silent battle of social supremacy played out in the space of a heartbeat.

Reginald suppressed a sigh. These social niceties were a necessary evil, he reminded himself. Appearances must be maintained, connections cultivated. It was all part of the intricate dance of business and society.

As they crossed the threshold into the church, the rich scent of pine and beeswax enveloped them. Reginald allowed himself a moment to appreciate the beauty of the sanctuary, decked out in its Christmas finery.

Reginald followed the usher down the aisle, his wife's hand resting lightly on his arm. The polished pews gleamed in the candlelight. As they approached their usual seats near the front, Reginald felt his business concerns and social obligations begin to slip away.

The usher stepped aside with a respectful nod, and Reginald allowed Beatrice to slide into the pew first. As he settled beside her, his eyes roamed over the festive garlands adorning the pillars and the wreath hanging above the altar.

For a moment, Reginald's mind drifted to his childhood. He recalled the excitement of Christmas Eve services, the anticipation of presents and family gatherings, the story of Baby Jesus sent to save the world. A faint smile tugged at the corners of his mouth, quickly hidden behind his usual stoic expression.

Beatrice sat ramrod straight beside him, her face a mask of stern composure. She smoothed invisible wrinkles from her skirt, her eyes darting around the church to assess who else had arrived. Reginald noticed her gaze lingering on Lady Havisham yet again, seated across the aisle.

As the organist began to play a soft prelude, Reginald felt an unusual sense of peace settle over him. The familiar melodies and the warmth of the church seemed to push aside thoughts of ledgers and business deals. He found himself genuinely looking forward to the service.

Beatrice turned her head, casting a cursory glance towards the choir loft. Her lips pressed into a thin line, and she leaned closer to Reginald.

"I don't see the usual choirmaster," she whispered. "I do hope they haven't allowed just anyone to lead the music tonight."

Reginald made a noncommittal sound, his attention drawn to the gentle flickering of the candles on the altar. For once, he was content to let the evening unfold without his usual need for control.

Reverend Thornton rose and made his way to the altar. The vicar's frailty was evident, his once-robust frame now bent with age and illness. Yet, as Thornton raised his hands to begin the service, a hush fell over the congregation.

As the Reverend's voice filled the church, Reginald noticed Beatrice fidgeting beside him. Her eyes darted towards the choir loft, a slight frown creasing her brow. Reginald followed her gaze, curious despite himself.

The usual choirmaster was indeed absent. In his place stood a young man Reginald vaguely recognised – wasn't he a clerk from Hardcastle's firm? Edward, that was his name. Beside him was a young woman with auburn hair, her face alight with an inner radiance that caught Reginald off guard.

Beatrice leaned close and whispered to her husband. "That's the scullery maid! What on earth is she doing up there?"

Reginald blinked, surprised. He rarely paid attention to the servants, but now that Beatrice mentioned it, he did recall glimpsing the girl around the manor. Clara, wasn't it? He'd never seen her like this, though – poised and confident, her eyes shining with purpose.

Reverend Thornton finished his introductions, and motioned to the choir with a smile.

As Edward raised his hands to lead the choir, Reginald found himself leaning forward slightly, intrigued despite his usual indifference to such matters. There was something in the air, a sense of expectancy that he couldn't quite explain.

The congregation held its collective breath, waiting for the first notes to fill the church.

As the opening notes of "*O Holy Night*" started, Clara's voice rose, clear and pure, soaring above the congregation. The effect was immediate and profound.

A hush fell over the church, as if every soul present held their breath in wonder. Reginald felt something stir deep within him, a long-forgotten emotion he couldn't quite name. The sheer beauty of Clara's voice caught him entirely off guard.

Her melody wove through the air, each note imbued with raw emotion that seemed to touch every heart in the room. Reginald found himself utterly captivated. He'd heard professional singers in London's finest opera houses, yet none had moved him like this simple girl's voice.

As Clara's song swelled, Reginald felt a strange tightness in his chest. He blinked rapidly, surprised to find moisture gathering in his eyes. The realisation dawned on him slowly, like the first rays of sunlight creeping over the horizon: this extraordinary talent had been right under his nose, unnoticed and unappreciated within his own household.

Beside him, Beatrice shifted uncomfortably. Her sharp whisper cut through the music. "Reginald, that girl up there – it's the scullery maid that abandoned her errands!"

Reginald raised a hand, gently shushing his wife. For once, he paid no heed to Beatrice's indignation. His entire being was focused on Clara's voice, on the way it filled the church with a transcendent beauty he'd never known existed in his own home.

A wave of shame washed over him. He thought of the countless times he'd walked past Clara without a word, treating her as little more than part of the furniture. How many other gifts had he overlooked in his relentless pursuit of wealth and status?

Reginald's hands clenched in his lap as memories flooded back – his own childhood dreams, long buried under expectations and ambition. He'd once loved music too, finding solace in the simple joy of a well-played melody. When had he lost that part of himself?

Clara's voice reached a crescendo, and Reginald felt a tear slide down his cheek. He didn't bother to wipe it away, too overwhelmed by the emotions coursing through him. In that moment, he saw Clara not as a servant, but as a young woman of immense talent and potential.

A sense of responsibility settled over him like a mantle. He had the power to right the wrongs of his previous neglect.

As the final notes of the hymn faded away, Reginald found himself changed. The hard shell of indifference he'd cultivated over years of business dealings had cracked, revealing a glimmer of the man he might have been – the man he could still become.

THE CHRISTMAS HYMN

Clara's voice soared as she began the next hymn, her heart swelling with a joy she hadn't felt in years. The rest of the choir joined in, their voices blending harmoniously with hers. The sound filled the church, wrapping around the congregation.

As she sang, Clara's gaze drifted to Reverend Thornton. Despite his obvious frailty, he sat upright in his chair, a serene smile playing on his face. His eyes shone with pride and contentment, a silent blessing for the reunion unfolding before him. Clara felt a rush of gratitude for the man who had first recognised her talent and given her a chance to shine.

Her eyes then found Edward, sitting tall and proud as he played the organ. Their gazes locked, and the world seemed to fall away. In that moment, Clara saw not just the boy she had known, but the man he had become. His eyes held a depth of emotion that took her breath away.

As they moved through the hymn, Clara and Edward's glances continued to meet and linger. Each look was charged with unspoken feelings – joy at their reunion, regret for the years lost, and a blossoming love that had grown from the seeds of their childhood friendship. Clara felt her heart quicken with each shared glance, a warmth spreading through her chest that had nothing to do with the exertion of singing.

The music swelled around them, but for Clara, it faded into the background. All she could focus on was Edward's steady gaze, the way his hands moved as he conducted with his left hand quickly before returning it to the organ's keys, and the subtle smile that formed whenever their eyes met. In those moments, she knew that whatever hardships lay behind them, whatever challenges might lie ahead, they would face them together.

As the final notes of the second hymn faded away, the church fell silent, a palpable stillness settling over the congregation. Clara could feel every eye upon her, but for once, she didn't shrink from the attention. Instead, she stood tall, her chest rising and falling with each breath, her cheeks flushed with exertion and joy.

The silence stretched for a heartbeat, then two. Clara's gaze found Edward's yet again, his eyes shining with pride and something deeper. Then, as if a dam had broken, applause erupted throughout the church. It started softly at first, then grew in volume and intensity until it filled every corner of the sacred space.

Clara felt overwhelmed by the outpouring of appreciation. She had sung in this church before, years ago, but never had she experienced such a response. The applause washed over her, erasing years of doubt and hardship. For a moment, she wasn't Clara the lowly maid or Clara the orphan. She was simply Clara.

Clara's gaze fell upon Mr and Mrs Flint. Mr Flint's face was a mask of astonishment, while Mrs Flint... Clara couldn't quite read the expression on her mistress's face.

AFTER THE SERVICE

Clara stood in the church vestibule, her heart racing as members of the congregation approached her and Edward. The warmth of their praise washed over her, a stark contrast to the coldness she'd grown accustomed to at Flint Manor.

"Your voice is simply angelic, my dear," an elderly woman gushed, clasping Clara's hands in her own.

"Thank you," Clara murmured, her cheeks flushing with pleasure.

She glanced at Edward, who stood beside her, beaming with pride. His hand found the small of her back, a gentle touch that sent a thrill through her. Clara felt stronger with him by her side, their shared smiles a silent promise of unity.

As the crowd thinned, Clara noticed Mr Flint approaching, his expression one of wonder and respect.

"Miss Winters," he began, his voice uncharacteristically gentle. "I... I had no idea you possessed such talent. Your singing was truly remarkable."

Clara blinked, surprised by the compliment. "Thank you, Mr Flint," she replied, her voice steady despite her racing heart.

THE ORPHAN'S CHRISTMAS HYMN

Before Mr Flint could continue, Mrs Flint appeared at his side, her face a mask of barely concealed fury. She tugged at her husband's arm, refusing to meet Clara's gaze.

"Come, Reginald," she hissed. "We must be going."

Clara saw her opportunity. Quickly, she retrieved the packages from her earlier errand and held them out to Mrs Flint.

"Your items from the market, ma'am. Apologies they're a bit late, but I'm sure Cook won't mind," Clara said.

Mrs Flint's eyes widened in shock, her mouth opening and closing wordlessly as she stared at the packages. Before she could regain her composure, Mr Flint took the packages from Clara.

"Thank you," he said swiftly, glancing at his wife, "we're happy to take these home with us. Please, do stay longer. I'll have the carriage come and pick you up later."

Clara was stunned by his kindness, but before she could properly respond Reverend Thornton appeared at her side.

"Ah, Miss Winters," he said warmly. "Might I have a word with you?" He gently took Clara's arm, leading her away from the stunned Mrs Flint.

As they walked, Clara felt a weight lifting from her shoulders. For the first time in years, she dared to hope for a future beyond the confines of Flint Manor.

∽

As the last few parishioners filed out of the church, their voices fading into the winter night, Clara was drawn to the altar. The flickering candlelight cast a warm glow over the polished wood, creating an intimate atmosphere that seemed to cocoon her and Edward from the outside world.

Edward gently took her hand, leading her to a nearby bench. They sat close, their shoulders touching, a comforting warmth spreading between them. Clara's heart fluttered as she looked at

Edward, his face illuminated by the soft light. His eyes, so full of warmth and affection, met hers.

"Clara," he said, "I can't believe how close we came to losing each other." He squeezed her hand. "But I promise you, whatever comes next, we'll face it together."

Clara felt tears welling up in her eyes, but for once, they were tears of joy. She blinked them back, not wanting to miss a moment of Edward's face.

"I've dreamed of this moment for so long," Edward continued. "Being here with you, hearing your voice again... it's like coming home." He raised her hand to his lips, pressing a gentle kiss to her knuckles. "I love you, Clara. I always have, and I always will."

Clara had imagined hearing those words so many times during her lonely nights at Flint Manor, but the reality was infinitely sweeter.

"Oh, Edward," she whispered, her voice trembling slightly. "I love you too. So much." She leaned her forehead against his, closing her eyes and savouring the moment. "Whatever happens, whatever we have to face, we'll do it side by side."

As they sat there, bathed in the warm glow of candles and newfound hope, Clara felt a peace she hadn't known in years. The future was uncertain, but with Edward by her side, she felt ready to face anything.

Clara stepped out of the church, her hand clasped tightly in Edward's. The cold night air nipped at her cheeks, but she hardly felt it. The warmth of Edward's presence and the glow of their newly professed love seemed to create a bubble of comfort around them.

Snowflakes danced in the lamplight, transforming the ordinary street into a wonderland. Clara looked up at Edward, marvelling at how the flakes caught in his dark hair, making it sparkle.

"It's beautiful," Clara murmured, gesturing to the snow-covered scene before them.

Edward smiled. "Not as beautiful as you."

A blush crept up her cheeks, and she ducked her head, still unused to such open affection. The sound of hooves on cobblestone drew her attention, and she looked up to see a carriage rounding the corner.

"That must be for you," Edward said, a hint of reluctance in his voice.

Clara nodded, her heart sinking a little at the thought of leaving Edward's side. But as she watched the carriage approach, she realised something had fundamentally changed. The vehicle that had once represented her captivity at Flint Manor now seemed like a chariot of possibility.

"It doesn't feel like an ending anymore," Clara said softly. "It feels like a beginning."

Edward squeezed her hand. "That's because it is, my love. We have so much ahead of us."

As the carriage drew to a stop before them, Clara turned to face Edward fully. The heavy snowfall created a curtain around them, as if nature itself was giving them a moment of privacy. Clara reached up, brushing a snowflake from Edward's cheek.

"I never want to forget this moment," she whispered.

BRIGHTER DAYS

Clara stood in the corner of the dining room, her hands clasped behind her back as she waited to serve breakfast. The morning light filtered through the windows, casting light shadows on the polished wood of the grand table. Mr Flint sat at the head, his newspaper folded neatly beside his plate.

As the staff filed in to attend to their duties, Mr Flint cleared his throat.

"I have some announcements to make," Mr Flint said, his voice carrying across the room. "Firstly, I wanted to wish you all a very merry Christmas. But more importantly, from this day forward, Clara Winters is to be treated with the utmost kindness and respect by all members of this household."

Clara's eyes widened. She glanced around, noting the surprised expressions on the faces of her fellow servants.

Mr Flint's gaze swept the room, his tone brooking no argument. "This is not a request, but a command. I expect everyone to comply without question."

A hushed murmur rippled through the gathered staff. Clara caught sight of Betsy and Mary exchanging hopeful glances, while Miss Crabtree seemed to breath a small sigh of relief.

As the staff dispersed to their duties, Clara overheard whispered conversations. "Did you hear that?" Betsy whispered to Thomas. "I wonder what's brought this on."

Before Clara could process the enormity of Mr Flint's proclamation, Mrs Flint burst into the room, her face flushed with anger.

"Reginald!" she hissed, her eyes flashing. "What is the meaning of this? That girl abandoned her duties last night, and now you're rewarding her?"

Mr Flint calmly set down his teacup, meeting his wife's gaze. "Beatrice, the errand you sent Clara on was needlessly cruel. It's time we put an end to such spiteful behaviour."

Mrs Flint's mouth opened and closed, her indignation palpable. "But—"

"No, Beatrice," Mr Flint cut her off, his voice firm but not unkind. "We must show more compassion and fairness to those in our employ. Clara has endured enough."

Mrs Flint's face flushed crimson, a mix of fury and humiliation etched across her features. The woman's lips pressed into a thin line, her eyes darting between her husband and Clara. For a moment, Clara thought Mrs Flint might erupt into one of her infamous tirades, but instead, she merely clenched her fists at her sides and stormed out of the room.

Over the next few days, Clara noticed a subtle shift in Mrs Flint's behaviour. The constant stream of criticism slowed to a trickle, and while Mrs Flint's gaze still held a hint of resentment, she no longer went out of her way to make Clara's life miserable. It was as if a dam had broken, dissolving years of pent-up bitterness.

The change rippled through the household like a stone cast into still water. Clara felt the tension ease from her shoulders as she went about her daily tasks. The other staff members, too, seemed to stand a little taller, their movements less hurried and anxious.

Even Miss Crabtree's and Mr Phineas' demeanours softened. Miss Crabtree still maintained her strict standards, but her instructions came without the usual barbed edge, and Mr Phineas would always find the time to congratulate Clara on a job well done. Clara found herself able to complete her chores without the constant fear of reprimand hanging over her head.

As Clara made her way through the house, she noticed small changes everywhere. The air felt lighter, the rooms brighter. For the first time since arriving at Flint Manor, she dared to hope that better days might lie ahead.

∼

Clara hummed softly to herself, a habit she'd never quite managed to break despite Mrs Flint's constant admonishments, and now she could do so freely.

The sound of footsteps echoed in the hallway, growing louder as they approached. Clara straightened, expecting to see Miss Crabtree with another list of tasks. Instead, Mr Flint appeared in the doorway, his imposing figure softened by an uncharacteristic hesitance.

"Miss Winters," he said, clearing his throat. "Might I have a word?"

Clara's heart quickened. She nodded, setting aside her cleaning cloth. "Of course, sir."

Mr Flint stepped into the room, his hands clasped behind his back. He seemed to struggle for words, a far cry from his usual commanding presence.

"I owe you an apology, Miss Winters," he finally said, his voice low and sincere. "I've been remiss in my duties as master of this house. Your treatment here has been... less than ideal, and for that, I am truly sorry."

Clara blinked, stunned by the unexpected admission. She opened her mouth to speak, but Mr Flint held up a hand.

"Please, let me finish. I failed to recognise your talent and worth. It was a grave oversight on my part."

He produced a small, leather-bound book from behind his back. "This is for you," he said, offering it to Clara. "A new hymnal. I hope it will serve as a reminder that your voice deserves to be heard."

Clara's fingers trembled as she accepted the gift. The leather was soft and supple, the gold lettering on the cover gleaming in the fading light.

"Thank you, sir," she said. "This is... very kind of you."

Mr Flint nodded, a ghost of a smile touching his lips. "It's the least I can do."

Clara clutched the hymnal to her chest, overwhelmed by the gesture. "I don't know what to say, sir. Thank you."

∽

CLARA'S HEART leaped with joy as Edward's familiar figure appeared at the gates of Flint Manor. His visits had become a cherished gift, a reminder of the strength she'd discovered within herself. As they strolled through the gardens, their fingers intertwined, Clara felt a surge of hope for the future they were building together.

Sundays became Clara's sanctuary. The familiar hymns washed over her as she stood in the choir loft, her voice soaring alongside her fellow singers. Mr Flint's unexpected kindness had opened this door, and Clara embraced it wholeheartedly.

After one particularly moving service, Reverend Thornton beckoned Clara and Edward to his study. Though his body was frail, his eyes shone with warmth and wisdom.

"My dear children," he said, his voice soft but steady. "I'm so proud of the strength you've shown. Clara, your ability to forgive and find joy in music again is truly inspiring."

Clara felt tears prick her eyes. "It hasn't always been easy, Reverend. But your guidance has been a light in dark times."

Reverend Thornton nodded. "Remember, forgiveness is not just for others, but for ourselves as well. Let your faith and your love for each other be your compass."

EDWARD'S COMMITMENT

"Clara, I've made a decision," Edward said, his voice steady and resolute. "I'm going to become a choirmaster. It's time I reignite my passion for music and take on a leadership role in the church."

Clara's heart swelled with pride and joy. She reached out, taking Edward's hands in hers. "Oh, Edward! That's wonderful news. I've always known you had it in you."

"It won't be easy," Edward admitted, a hint of uncertainty creeping into his voice. "There's so much to learn, so much to overcome. But Mr Flint has said he'll aid in paying for my father's treatment, which means I can go back to music."

Clara squeezed his hands reassuringly. "That is so kind of Mr Flint! And I'll be right here beside you, every step of the way. We'll face whatever challenges come, together."

As the seasons changed, so too did Clara and Edward's relationship. They spent countless hours in the church, their voices blending in perfect harmony as they practiced hymns and explored new musical compositions each Sunday. Edward's confidence grew with each passing day, his natural talent for leadership shining through as he guided the choir.

On some quiet afternoons, they would sit in the garden at Flint Manor, discussing their hopes and dreams for the future. Clara found herself opening up about the hardships she had faced, and Edward listened with unwavering support and understanding.

"You're the strongest person I know, Clara," Edward said one day, his eyes filled with admiration. "Your faith and resilience inspire me every day."

"And you, Edward, remind me of the beauty and joy that music can bring to life. Together, we're unstoppable."

As spring blossoms gave way to summer sunshine, Clara and Edward's love deepened. They found solace in each other's company, their shared faith providing a strong foundation for their relationship.

THE REVEREND'S MEMORY

Clara stood by Edward's side as Reverend Thornton's health deteriorated. When the end came, she held Edward as he wept, her own tears falling silently. She murmured words of comfort, her voice steady despite the ache in her chest. "He's at peace now, Edward. Your father knew how much you loved him."

The day of the funeral dawned crisp and clear. Clara smoothed her black dress, took a deep breath, and made her way to the church. As she stood before the congregation, her eyes found Edward's grief-stricken face. She began to sing, her voice rich with emotion, carrying the sorrow and love that filled the room.

The notes of "*Amazing Grace*" soared through the church, Clara's voice a balm to the mourners' hearts. She poured every ounce of her being into the hymn, honouring Reverend Thornton's memory and offering solace to those he left behind. As the final notes faded, a sense of peace settled over the assembly.

In the days that followed, Clara watched as determination slowly replaced the sorrow in Edward's eyes. He spoke of his father's unwavering support, of the legacy he wanted to honour.

"I'm going to become the choirmaster my father always believed I could be," Edward told her, his voice firm with resolve.

Pride filled Clara's heart. "And I'll be right here to help you, every step of the way."

Clara watched Edward with pride and love as he threw himself into his new role as choirmaster. His dedication reminded her of his father, and she felt a bittersweet pang at the thought of Reverend Thornton. The man who had believed in her, who had given her a chance when no one else would, was gone. But his legacy lived on in Edward's determination and in the music that filled the church each Sunday.

As the weeks passed, Clara found herself spending as much time as she could at the church, helping Edward prepare for services and rehearsals. She relished these moments, when it was just the two of them in the quiet sanctuary, their voices blending in perfect harmony as they practiced hymns.

She also loved attending the services each Sunday morning, singing whenever she could, and discussing the sermon with Edward as they walked through town afterwards.

One day during rehearsals, Clara paused in her singing to watch Edward at the organ. His brow was furrowed in concentration, his fingers dancing over the keys with growing confidence. She remembered the boy who had once snuck her sheet music at the orphanage.

"You're becoming quite the choirmaster," Clara said softly as Edward finished playing.

He turned to her, smiling. "I couldn't do it without you, Clara. Your voice, your understanding of music... it's invaluable."

Clara felt a blush creep up her cheeks. "We make a good team, don't we?"

Edward nodded, his eyes holding hers. "We always have."

In that moment, surrounded by the echoes of their music

and the memories of all they'd been through, a sense of rightness settled over Clara. This was where she belonged – not just in the church, but by Edward's side, their voices and lives intertwined.

A CHRISTMAS EVE SURPRISE

*E*dward felt a thrill of excitement as he walked through the bustling streets of Dorking. The town had transformed into a winter wonderland once again, with wreaths adorning every door and garlands strung across shop windows. The air was thick with the promise of snow, and the scent of cinnamon and pine wafted from nearby bakeries and street vendors.

He clutched his bag with increasing fervour. The weight of what was inside felt both terrifying and exhilarating. Edward had spent weeks agonising over the perfect moment, and now, with Christmas Eve approaching, he knew the time had finally come.

As he entered St. Paul's Church, Edward was greeted by the sight of Clara directing a group of volunteers in hanging holly and mistletoe. Her cheeks were flushed with exertion, her eyes bright with joy. She caught sight of him and beamed, causing Edward's heart to skip a beat.

"Edward! Thank goodness you're here. We need your expert opinion on the choir arrangement."

He chuckled, making his way through the sea of decorations. "I'm not sure how expert my opinion is, but I'll do my best."

∼

THE CHURCH GLOWED with the warm light of countless candles. Clara stood at the front of the choir, her heart full of joy as she led the congregation in singing beloved Christmas hymns. Edward stood beside her, his rich baritone blending perfectly with her clear soprano. This year he had decided to sing alongside her.

As they sang "*O Holy Night*," Clara felt a sense of peace and belonging wash over her. She glanced at Edward, catching his eye, and they shared a smile. The trials of the past few years seemed to melt away in the face of their love and the beauty of the music.

When the final notes of the last hymn faded away, Reverend Matthews stepped forward to deliver the benediction. Clara expected the service to end as it always did, with the congregation filing out into the snowy night. But as people began to rise from their seats, Edward touched her arm gently.

"Wait here a moment," he whispered, a hint of nervousness in his voice.

Clara watched, puzzled, as Edward strode to the front of the church. He cleared his throat, and the murmur of voices died down.

"If I could have everyone's attention for just a moment more," Edward said, his voice carrying through the church. "There's something I'd like to do before we all depart."

He beckoned Clara forward, and she felt her cheeks grow warm as all eyes turned to her. Edward reached into his coat pocket and pulled out a small, leather-bound book.

"Clara," he said, his voice trembling slightly. "This is for you."

Clara took the book, running her fingers over the embossed

title: "Hymns of the Heart." She looked up at Edward, touched by the thoughtful gift.

"Open it," he urged softly.

As Clara lifted the cover, she gasped. Nestled in a hollow cut into the pages was a ring, its diamond catching the candlelight and sparkling brilliantly. Tears sprang to her eyes as she realised what was happening.

Edward took her hand in his, his eyes shining with love and hope. "Clara Winters," he began, his voice filled with emotion. "You have been the song in my heart since the day we met. Will you do me the great honour of becoming my wife?"

For a moment, Clara couldn't find her voice, overwhelmed by the love shining in Edward's eyes and the significance of this moment.

"Yes," she finally managed. Then, louder, "Yes, Edward. I will marry you!"

Edward's face broke into a radiant smile as he slipped the ring onto Clara's finger. The church erupted in applause and cheers, the sound echoing off the stone walls and filling the space with jubilation.

Clara threw her arms around Edward's neck, and he lifted her off her feet in a joyous embrace. As he set her down, she pressed her forehead to his, savouring the moment.

"I love you," she murmured, her words meant only for him despite the excited chatter around them.

"And I love you," Edward replied.

As they turned to face the congregation, Clara felt a surge of joy at the sight of so many familiar faces beaming at them. Old John from Flint Manor wiped a tear from his weathered cheek. Cook was practically bouncing with excitement, while Betsy and Mary clasped hands, their faces alight with happiness for their friend.

Even Mr and Mrs Flint were present, Mr Flint nodding

approvingly while Mrs Flint wore an expression that, while not quite a smile, lacked its usual harshness.

Reverend Matthews stepped forward, raising his hands for quiet. "Let us all join in blessing this union," he said, his voice ringing out clear and strong.

As the reverend spoke words of blessing over them, Clara leaned into Edward's embrace. For the first time since losing her parents, Clara knew she was with her family.

PLANS FOR THE FUTURE

Clara's heart soared as she and Edward left the church hand in hand, their fingers intertwined. The cool night air kissed their flushed cheeks, but Clara barely noticed, warmed by the love that radiated between them. As they walked through the snow-dusted streets, their breaths visible in the frosty air, Clara couldn't stop glancing at the ring that now adorned her finger.

"I can hardly believe it," she whispered, her voice filled with wonder. "We're engaged."

Edward squeezed her hand gently. "Believe it, my love. This is just the beginning of our life together."

They found a quiet bench in the town square, brushing off the snow before sitting down. Clara nestled close to Edward, drawing comfort from his warmth and strength.

"What do you think about a Christmas wedding next year?" Edward asked, his eyes twinkling with excitement. "It would give us time to plan and prepare."

Clara nodded enthusiastically. "That sounds perfect. A whole year to dream and plan our future together."

As they sat there, surrounded by the twinkling lights of the town's Christmas decorations, Clara and Edward began to share their hopes and dreams for their life together. They spoke of music, of course – how they would fill their home with melodies and harmonies, how they would continue to serve in the church choir, and how they might even start a small music school for underprivileged children.

"We could use the skills we've learned," Clara mused, "to bring joy and hope to others through music, just as it's brought us together."

Edward nodded, his face alight with enthusiasm. "And we'll make our home a haven of love and faith," he added. "A place where we can grow together in our love for each other and for God."

As they continued to talk, peace settled over Clara. The hardships she had endured at St Mary's and Flint Manor seemed to fade into the background, overshadowed by the bright future that lay ahead. She knew there would be challenges, but with Edward by her side and their shared faith to guide them, she felt ready to face whatever life might bring.

A CHANGE

As August approached, Clara found herself in a reflective mood. She stood by the window of her small attic room at Flint Manor, gazing out at the changing leaves in the garden. The past few years had been a crucible, testing her spirit and resolve in ways she never could have imagined when she first arrived as a frightened, heartbroken girl.

Clara ran her fingers along the worn spine of her first hymnal, the gift from her parents. It was a tangible reminder of how far she'd come. The hardships she'd endured – Mrs Flint's cruelty, the backbreaking work, the isolation – had forged her into someone stronger, more resilient. She'd discovered depths of courage and determination she never knew she possessed.

Yet as she looked around the sparse room that had been her sanctuary, Clara knew it was time for change. Her heart quickened at the thought of pursuing her true passion – teaching music to children who might otherwise never have the opportunity to learn. Mr Flint's offer of financial assistance to help her establish herself independently before the wedding touched her deeply, a final act of kindness to make amends for the past. They had found her a small cottage just on the edge of town, where she would reside and work before her upcoming wedding.

Later that evening, Clara met Edward in their favourite spot in the church garden. As twilight painted the sky in soft hues, she shared her decision to leave Flint Manor and move into town.

"It feels right," Clara said, her voice filled with quiet conviction. "These months before our wedding, I want to start building the life we've dreamed of."

Edward's eyes shone with pride and love. He took her hands in his, his touch warm and reassuring. "I think it's a wonderful idea, Clara. You've more than earned the chance to spread your wings."

They sat in companionable silence for a moment, both contemplating the future that stretched before them. Clara felt a mix of excitement and nervous anticipation, but Edward's steadfast support buoyed her spirits.

"We'll face whatever comes together," Edward said softly, echoing her thoughts. "This is just the beginning of our journey."

Clara nodded, a smile spreading across her face. She was ready to embrace this new chapter, to step fully into the person she'd become through trials and triumphs alike.

FAREWELL TO THE FLINT ESTATE

Clara Winters moved through the halls of Flint Manor with a sense of purpose, her steps measured and deliberate. She'd spent the past week meticulously preparing for her departure, ensuring every task was completed to perfection. As she polished the last of the silver, her mind wandered to the countless times she'd performed this duty, her fingers now moving almost of their own accord.

In the kitchen, Clara carefully went over the linen inventory with Charlotte, the new maid, explaining the particular preferences of each family member. "Mrs Flint likes the napkins pressed just so," she said, demonstrating the precise fold. Charlotte thanked her. Clara had seen Betsy watching her instruct, misty eyed, no doubt remembering how Betsy had done the same for Clara years ago.

Clara then sought out Thomas, finding him in the butler's pantry. She handed him a neatly written poem. She knew he preferred small and silent gestures of kindness and affection. Thomas took the poem with a solemn nod, his usual stoicism softened by a hint of sadness.

In the garden, Clara found Old John tending to the roses.

She knelt beside him, helping to prune the delicate blooms one last time. "You've taught me so much about finding beauty in unexpected places," she said softly. Old John's weathered hand patted hers gently, a lifetime of wisdom in his kind eyes.

As evening approached, Clara made her way to the kitchen, where Cook was preparing the staff's dinner. The familiar scents of home-cooked meals enveloped her, bringing a lump to her throat. "I'll miss your cooking terribly," Clara said.

Cook turned from the stove, her round face creased with a bittersweet smile. "Oh, my dear girl," she said, pulling Clara into a warm embrace. "You've been a ray of sunshine in this old kitchen. Promise you'll visit and let me fatten you up now and then."

Clara nodded, unable to speak past the tightness in her throat. She looked around at the gathered staff – Cook, Betsy, Mary, Thomas, and Old John – each face etched with a mix of joy for her future and sorrow at her leaving. Even Miss Crabtree and Mr Phineas gave her nods of approval as they said their goodbyes.

"I can't thank you all enough," Clara began, her voice wavering slightly. "Your kindness, your friendship... it's meant more to me than I can say. You've been my family here, and I'll carry you in my heart always."

∽

CLARA TOOK A DEEP BREATH, smoothing her skirts as she approached Mr Flint's study. She knocked softly, her heart pounding.

"Enter," Mr Flint's voice called from within.

Clara stepped into the room, her eyes adjusting to the dim light. Mr Flint sat behind his imposing desk, while Mrs. Flint perched stiffly in an armchair by the window.

"Ah, Clara," Mr Flint said. "I understand you're leaving us today."

Clara nodded, clasping her hands in front of her. "Yes, sir. I wanted to express my gratitude for the opportunity you've given me."

Mr Flint waved away her thanks. "Nonsense, my dear. It is we who should be thanking you. Your voice... well, it's opened my eyes to many things." He leaned forward, his eyes twinkling. "I can't wait to see what you'll accomplish, Clara. You have a bright future ahead of you."

Clara was so grateful for Mr Flint's kind and thoughtful words.

She turned to Mrs Flint, who sat rigidly, her gaze fixed on the window. "Mrs Flint," Clara began, her voice soft but steady. "I wanted to thank you as well."

Mrs Flint's eyes flickered to Clara's face, then away again. She remained silent, her lips pressed into a thin line.

Clara took a step closer, her heart full of unexpected compassion. "I truly wish you peace, Mrs Flint," she said, her voice carrying a sincerity that filled the room. "I hope that you can find the happiness and satisfaction you so deserve."

Mrs Flint's head snapped up, her eyes widening in surprise. For a moment, the mask of indifference slipped, revealing a flicker of something – perhaps regret, or a grudging respect. Though she didn't speak, Clara saw the impact of her words in the slight softening of Mrs Flint's features.

⁓

Clara stepped out of the Flint estate, her small bag of belongings clutched in one hand. The sun peeked through the clouds, casting a warm glow on the path before her. She paused at the gate, looking back at the imposing manor house that had been her home for so long.

A whirlwind of emotions swept through her – relief, gratitude, and a touch of melancholy. The weight of years spent scrubbing floors and enduring Mrs Flint's sharp tongue seemed to lift from her shoulders with each step away from the house.

Clara took a deep breath, inhaling the scent of freedom and new beginnings. The air tasted sweeter somehow, filled with promise and possibility. She thought of the little cottage Mr Flint had provided, where she would soon begin teaching music to local children. A smile tugged at her lips as she imagined filling those rooms with song.

There stood Edward, his familiar figure a beacon of hope and love. He beamed at her, his eyes shining with pride and affection.

"Ready for your new adventure, my love?" Edward asked, extending his hand.

Clara's fingers intertwined with his, the touch grounding her in the present moment. "More than ready," she replied, her voice steady and sure.

Together, they took their first steps away from the Flint estate. Anticipation rose in Clara, tinged with nervous energy. The path ahead was unknown, but with Edward by her side, she felt ready to face whatever challenges lay ahead.

As they walked towards the cart Edward had borrowed, Clara's mind drifted to the music school they dreamed of opening, to the home they would build together filled with love and laughter. The future stretched out before them, bright and full of promise.

A NEW CHAPTER

◈

Clara stood before the small group of children gathered in her cottage, her heart racing with nervous excitement. She smoothed her simple cotton dress, steadying herself. This was it—the moment she'd been dreaming of for so long.

"Welcome, everyone," she said, her voice warm and inviting. "I'm Miss Winters, and today we're going to embark on a wonderful journey through music."

The children's faces ranged from eager to uncertain, reminding Clara of her own early days at St Mary's. She knelt down, meeting their eyes.

"Now, who here likes to sing?"

A few hands shot up, while others remained hesitant.

"That's alright," Clara assured them. "By the end of our time together, I bet you'll all be singing your hearts out."

She started with a simple melody, one her mother had taught her long ago. As Clara's clear voice filled the room, she saw the children's eyes widen. Even the most reluctant began to sway slightly to the rhythm.

"Let's try it together now," Clara encouraged. "Don't worry about getting it perfect. Just feel the music in your heart."

Slowly, tentatively, small voices joined hers. Clara beamed, remembering how music had been her solace during the darkest times at Flint Manor. She was determined to share that gift with these children.

As the lesson progressed, Clara drew on her experiences. When little Tommy struggled with a high note, she recalled Mrs Flint's harsh criticisms and chose a different approach.

"That's it, Tommy. You're so close," she said gently. "Let's try it once more, nice and easy."

The boy's face lit up as he hit the note, and Clara couldn't help but beam.

By the end of the class, the room rang with joyous, if slightly off-key, singing. Clara's cheeks hurt from smiling so much. As the children filed out, chattering excitedly, several parents approached her.

"Miss Winters, I've never seen Rachel so enthusiastic about anything," one mother said, her eyes shining. "Thank you."

Clara nodded. This was everything she'd hoped for and more.

Clara watched with pride as her small music class grew into something truly special. Word spread through the community about the joyful sounds emanating from Clara's Cottage, and soon children from all walks of life were clamouring to join.

She marvelled at the transformation in her students. Little Tommy, once shy and hesitant, now led the others with his clear, strong voice. Rachel, who had struggled to read music, beamed as she deciphered a new piece on her own.

"Remember," Clara told them one afternoon, her voice gentle but firm, "music is more than just notes on a page. It's about expressing what's in your heart."

The children nodded solemnly, their faces rapt with attention.

As the weeks passed, Clara noticed changes beyond just musical ability. Children who had once been withdrawn now laughed and played together during breaks. Others, previously prone to mischief, found focus and discipline in mastering their instruments.

Edward was a constant presence, his support unwavering. He'd arrive early to help set up chairs or stay late to discuss fundraising ideas. Sometimes, he'd sit at the piano, accompanying the children's voices with a tender smile that made Clara's heart swell.

One evening, as they tidied up after a particularly successful lesson, Edward turned to Clara.

"You know," he said softly, "watching you with those children... it's like seeing you come alive in a whole new way."

Clara felt her cheeks warm. "It's everything I dreamed of," she admitted. "Giving them the gift of music, helping them find their voices—just as others once did for me."

Edward took her hand, his eyes shining. "We're building something beautiful here, Clara. Not just music, but hope and belonging."

Clara nodded, too overcome to speak. As they stood there, surrounded by scattered sheet music and the lingering echoes of children's laughter, she knew that this was exactly where she was meant to be.

∼

CLARA'S STUDENTS took the stage at the town hall. Little Tommy, once so shy, now stood tall as he led the group in a rendition of "*Silent Night.*" The audience sat transfixed, many wiping away tears as the pure, sweet voices filled the air.

As the final notes faded, the hall erupted in applause. Clara's heart swelled with joy, remembering her own first performance at St Paul's so long ago. She caught Edward's eye in the crowd, his smile mirroring her own.

Word of the children's talents spread quickly through Dorking. Soon, Clara found herself fielding requests for performances at local events and even in neighbouring towns. With each success, more families sought out her tutelage, eager for their children to experience the transformative power of music.

One crisp winter morning, a letter arrived bearing the Flint family seal. Clara's hands trembled slightly as she opened it, memories of her time at the manor flooding back. Inside, she found a brief note from Mr Flint, along with a generous donation for musical instruments and sheet music.

"Your gift deserves to be shared," the note read. "May this help you continue your good work."

Clara pressed the paper to her chest, overcome with emotion. She thought of Mrs Flint, wondering if the bitter woman had found any peace. Perhaps, by being a kind and encouraging teacher, Clara was aiding in making sure what Mrs Flint went through didn't happen to more potential singers.

As December approached, Clara was caught up in a whirlwind of wedding preparations. She and Edward spent evenings poring over hymn selections and discussing their vows. Their shared passion for music infused every aspect of the planning, from the choir arrangements to the recessional.

"I never imagined I could be this happy," Clara confessed one night as they walked home from choir practice, their breath visible in the chilly air.

Edward squeezed her hand. "Nor did I. It's as if every hardship led us to this moment."

Clara nodded, thinking of the long journey that had brought them here. From the orphanage to Flint Manor, through separation and reunion, their love had not only endured but flourished.

THE WEDDING

Clara stood before the mirror in the small room adjacent to the church, her heart fluttering with anticipation. The white dress she wore was simple yet elegant, a gift from Mr Flint that had brought tears to her eyes when he presented it. She smoothed her hands over the fabric, hardly believing that this day had finally arrived.

A soft knock at the door drew her attention. "Come in," she called, her voice steady despite her nerves.

Betsy and Mary entered with beaming smiles. "Oh, Clara," Betsy breathed, "you look absolutely beautiful."

Clara embraced them both, grateful for their presence. "Thank you for being here," she said.

As they helped her with the final touches, Clara's mind wandered to Edward, waiting for her at the altar. She thought of their journey, the hardships they had overcome, and the love that had blossomed between them.

The church bells began to ring, signalling it was time. Clara took a deep breath, picked up her bouquet, and stepped into the hallway. Old John was there, looking dapper in a borrowed suit. He offered his arm with a gentle smile. "Ready, lass?"

Clara nodded. As they walked towards the church doors, she could hear the choir – her students – beginning to sing "*Silent Night*." The familiar melody washed over her, filling her with peace.

The doors opened, and Clara's breath caught in her throat. The church was filled with faces both familiar and new. She saw Cook dabbing at her eyes with her apron, Thomas standing tall and proud near the back, and even Miss Crabtree offering a small smile.

But it was Edward who captured her attention completely. He stood at the altar, his eyes shining with love and tears. As Clara walked down the aisle, their gazes locked, and the rest of the world seemed to fade away.

When she reached Edward, he took her hands in his, squeezing gently. "You're here," he whispered, his voice filled with wonder.

"I'm here," Clara replied, her heart overflowing with joy.

THE FIRST CHAPTER OF 'THE ORPHAN'S RESCUED NIECE'

BY DOROTHY WELLINGS

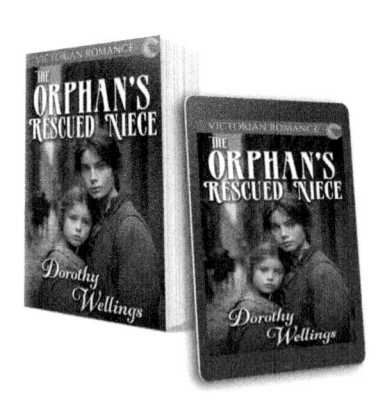

SOUTHWARK, LONDON, 1871

Beatrice Portly sat at the edge of the damp, mould-infested pavement waiting for her brother, Roy, who told her to not go anywhere otherwise he'd not be able to find her. Her brown shoes had thinned at the soles and water seeped between her toes as she kicked at the small puddles gathered in the potholes of Theed Street. She pulled her worn-out woollen coat to cover her nose. The smelly, unpleasant air was worse as the gutsy wind blew everything hither and thither in its path.

Oblivious to the wind, children from the neighbourhood laughed and kicked cans down the street, others built castles out of pebbles and rubble. Above the street, women were sharing stories as they hung wet clothes on ropes between the tenements. People had set up broken and chipped tables and chairs on the dire pavement in hopes of selling their wares.

Across the street, a middle-aged woman welcomed a man and a young boy covered in soot inside their house. She imagined it would be the same as their block. The five-story building with four tiny flats on each floor bulked with varied-sized families. She and Roy shared one room, Auntie Sadie slept on a cot in the corner of the living room cum kitchen, which had a table, three chairs and a cast iron stove with a grate.

"Hoi, why you sticking your feet in the water?"

Roy's croaky voice jammed in her ear as he sat beside her. His faded blue coat was thicker than when he'd left her earlier and his loosely-fitted cap was askew over his left ear.

"I'm bored. You were gone for hours," Beatrice said with a huff. "Next time I want to go with you."

"No, you can't."

"You always say that."

"It's 'cause you'll just get in the way."

"In the way of what?"

He grabbed her arm and pulled her to her feet. "Let's get home before Auntie Sadie does. She'll be in a dander if we're not there."

Beatrice side-glanced her brother with annoyance and noticed a shine inside his coat. She opened her mouth but knew better and said nothing. Roy grasped her hand and sprinted to the end of the street, squirming between narrow alleys until they crossed the Southwark Bridge over the dark, murky Thames River.

"Slow down," Beatrice said pulling her hand from her brother's grasp and said, "I can't run fast like you." She stopped and leaned over placing her palms over her knees, panting. Her mop hat fell to her soggy feet amidst the mushy ground and she seized it with a sigh. Aunt Sadie would reprimand her as she had cleaned it only yesterday.

"We're almost there, see?" Roy said, pointing to his left. "Down Park Street, turn a few corners and then we're in Red Cross. It's not far."

"For you," said Beatrice between breaths, covering her head with the soiled hat. "Lant Street is far."

"Don't dally. Auntie Sadie is coming through Piccadilly so we don't have much time."

"I wanted to go to school," Beatrice said lifting her chin with a scowl on her face. "What do you think she's gonna say when I tell her I didn't go."

"Nothing, you say nothing, but a fine day."

Roy snapped her hand into his and dragged her behind him slipping past stationery wagons and with the slight of his hand grabbed whatever he could as they passed merchants. Those who saw him were too late and offered words of obscenity waving angry fists in the air.

"Take this," he said, shoving a hunk of dry bread into her hand as they snuck into an alleyway.

Beatrice's stomach growled. She hadn't eaten all day. Though she knew where he got the bread from, she took it and guilt filled her as she ate it.

"Now hurry, let's go," Roy urged, tugging on her arm. "Please, Bea, you know Auntie Sadie gets home early when she works in Piccadilly."

With a massive nod and not wanting to disappoint her brother, she said, "Yes, let's go, Roy."

She grabbed hold of his hand and they scurried through the streets and arrived home just as Auntie Sadie ambled around the corner, her large shoulder strap bag dangling from her shoulder.

"Put on the stove, quick!" Beatrice yelled, stomping up the whittled staircase behind her brother to the third floor. "I'll peel potatoes."

Behind one of the doors adjacent to them, a baby wailed.

The door rattled as Roy pushed the door open and he stumbled over the rutted floor. While Beatrice hurried to the tiny box in the corner of the larder where they kept a table, Roy grabbed the flint on the floor near the stove and within minutes a soft glow radiated from it.

Rubbing their hands they heard the door creak open followed by shuffling. Beatrice bolted to the table and picked up a knife, her heart thumped. Would Auntie Sadie know? Grown-ups had a way of knowing things. Her mind raced thinking of what to tell her aunt.

Auntie Sadie limped into the living room where Roy greeted her at the door, took the bag from her and placed it onto her cot.

"Did you have a good day?" Auntie Sadie said with a smile in her voice, sitting on a wobbly back-slated chair that Roy had placed near the grate for her.

"Oh yes," Roy answered with a bright grin.

"Must I chop the potatoes?" Beatrice said from the minuscule larder, and she saw her aunt nod through the gaps between the rotting timeworn boards of wood. Auntie's eyes were droopy and her face weary.

"Why don't you rest," Roy offered. "I'll get more water and help Bea cook supper."

"Helpful today, aren't you?" Auntie Sadie said with a raised brow. She kicked off her shoes and slid the chair forward toward the grate. "Makes me think you're up to no good again."

Roy's face drained of colour and his eyes widened in mock horror. "No, I'm gonna get more water and…" his voice dropped, but added a hint of cheer, "I got some vegetables and fruit. They aren't too fresh, but we can boil them."

Auntie Sadie's brows knitted. "You went to the market again, didn't you?"

When Roy remained silent and his eyes hit the floor, Auntie Sadie clicked her tongue with disdain.

"Why do you think I work extra days cleaning houses?" she said in a warbled voice. "To get us by, that's why. Do you want the bobbies to take you to the workhouse?"

Roy shook his head and stared at her, "No, I don't want that. I only want to help."

"I don't want Roy to go to the workhouse," Beatrice said, tears pricking her eyes. "We'll never see each other."

"Then go to school," Auntie Sadie peered at them both. "You didn't go to school, did you?" she glared at Beatrice, who shook her head.

"I'm sorry, I'll go tomorrow. I promise." Beatrice's heart thumped harder. "Please don't send Roy away, he's not thirteen yet, he can still come to school."

Auntie Sadie turned away and stared at the warm, flickering glow with a sigh. "I don't want either of you to go there. It's not good for families to be split up." Pointing at her bag she said, "Look inside. The Hembley's have thrown out clothes and shoes. There's an old dress and shoes for you, Beatrice, throw out the ones you have now. Trousers and a shirt for you, Roy."

Beatrice and Roy stared at each other in delight and whooped.

"Thank you, thank you," said Beatrice rushing towards their auntie's bag with Roy close behind her.

"Stop, Roy," Auntie Sadie said, glaring at him. "Fetch the water first. Think twice before leaving your sister alone and now I have to wash her hat again."

Roy's lips tipped downward and his head bobbed. "I'm

sorry," he whispered and grabbed the pail before disappearing out the door.

Pain stabbed Beatrice's heart staring after him as she held onto the new dress, well, old, but it had no holes. She knew he meant well, but she wished her brother would listen. Roy, like many children, would steal and Auntie Sadie scolded him whenever she found out.

Beatrice pulled out two small black-heeled shoes. "Aunt Sadie, why do rich people throw out such nice things?" She inspected the shoes and decided they only needed a polish to shine.

Aunt Sadie rose to her feet. "Take off those shoes and dry your feet. You'll get sick. People get tired of the same clothes and want to look new and different."

"Would I look different in this new dress?" Beatrice said, holding up the dress to her shoulders, the hem stopped at her ankles.

Removing the grubby mop hat from Beatrice's head, Auntie Sadie planted a kiss on her head and said, "No, you're still pretty as you. You can't be anyone, but you. Go dry your feet and I'll take over supper."

Exaggerated *oofs* and *ah's* sounded from the door and Beatrice turned to her aunt giggling. She ran to the door and shifted it open for Roy staggering under the hefty weight of the pail, water spilling everywhere.

"Leave it by the door," Auntie Sadie said with a jerk of her head. "Try on the shirt and trousers, you're going to need them soon."

"What do you mean?" he said, digging inside her bag and pulling out brown trousers and a white cotton shirt with buttons.

"I'll tell you later," Auntie Sadie said.

"These are fancy, a bit big though. I'll grow into them, thank you."

Auntie Sadie walked to the pail of water and filled a pot to boil the potatoes. Turning to Roy she said, "Hand me those vegetables. You both look like waifs. We'll make do with the vegetables and have the fruit after supper."

Roy's face beamed and he dropped the clothes onto the cot. He dug into his coat and like a magician, he pulled out carrots and beans.

The Hembly's cook took a liking to Auntie Sadie and whenever there were leftovers, she shared them. Auntie Sadie had never looked happier announcing there'd be meat in the broth. She'd been given extra money and had bought fresh bread. Despite Auntie Sadie's disapproval, after supper, they'd enjoyed the apples and bananas Roy had provided.

With the candle burning on the stool in the living room, Beatrice loved hearing stories about the rich people and how they lived. Auntie Sadie told it like it was a fairytale. A house with rooms the size of their tenement and larger didn't sound real.

Auntie Sadie yawned and kissed them both on their cheeks. "I'll be going to sleep now. It's an early start to get to the Richardson House in Hyde Park. Don't stay up too late."

Once Auntie Sadie had gone to bed, Roy tapped Beatrice's hand and shoved something cool into her hand.

"Happy birthday," he said with a shy grin. "I'm sorry I couldn't get anything for you last week, but I couldn't find anything you'd like. You're nine now, practically a lady."

Beatrice's eyes widened with astonishment. Glancing from her brother to her hand, she was breathless. He'd given her a shiny brass bracelet in her hand with green, white, gold and pink beads.

"See, the green is like your eyes," his grin broadened, "the light pink is your hair. There are nine gold beads."

"Thank you," Beatrice stammered, choking over her words. It was the most beautiful thing she'd ever seen. "I love it, but-but

I can't keep this." She held it out to him. "Auntie Sadie would be angry if she knew."

His face turned solemn and he wrapped his hand over hers, pushing her hand back. "It's yours. You can't give away a present now, can you?"

"No, you're right," she said, shaking her head and tears gathered in her eyes. Leaning forward she embraced him. "I won't show Auntie Sadie. I'll keep it safe."

"Good," his bright grin returned. "Go sleep now. I need to meet up with some friends."

"But…it's night-time and—"

"Shush, Bea, you'll wake Auntie Sadie," he said covering her mouth with his forefinger. "I won't be late, promise. Go sleep now."

He hopped to his feet and gripped his coat, before hurrying out the door.

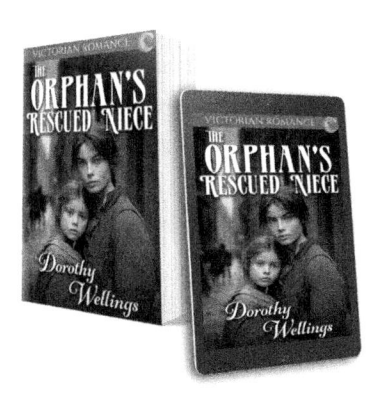

**Click here to read the rest of
'The Orphan's Rescued Niece'**

A tale of family, sacrifice, and the courage to choose a better future.

Beatrice Portly's life has been one of constant struggle and sacrifice. Orphaned at a young age, she and her brother Roy are raised by their kind-hearted Aunt Sadie in the unforgiving slums of Victorian London. As Beatrice grows from a wide-eyed child into a resilient young woman, she finds herself caught between her love for her troubled brother and her desire for a life free from poverty and fear.

When Roy's drinking spirals out of control, threatening not only himself but also his young daughter Sadie, Beatrice is forced to make an impossible choice. With the help of the compassionate Oscar Talloway, a man from a world far removed from her own, Beatrice must find the strength to forge a new path - not just for herself, but for her beloved niece as well.

As the shadows of her past threaten to engulf her, Beatrice discovers that sometimes the bravest thing one can do is to let go. Will she have the courage to break free from the cycle of poverty and addiction that has defined her life? And in doing so, can she open her heart to the possibility of love and a future she never dared to imagine?

'The Orphan's Rescued Niece'

OUR GIFT TO YOU

AS A WAY TO SAY THANK YOU WE WOULD LOVE TO SEND YOU THIS BEAUTIFUL STORY FREE OF CHARGE.

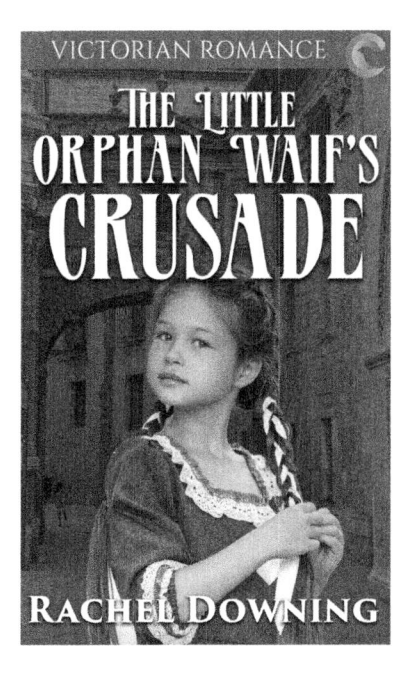

Click here for your FREE COPY of
'The Little Orphan Waif's Crusade'

CornerstoneTales.com/sign-up

In the wake of her father's passing, seven-year-old Matilda is determined to heal her sister Effie's shattered spirit.

Desperate to restore joy to Effie's life, Matilda embarks on a daring quest, aided by the gentle-hearted postman, Philip. Together, they weave a plan to ignite the flame of love in Effie's heart once more.

At Cornerstone Tales we publish books you can trust. Great tales without sex or swearing, but with all of the mystery and romance you expect from a great story.

Be the first to know when we release new books, take part in our fun competitions, and get surprise free books in your inbox by signing up to our free VIP Reader list.

As a thank you you'll receive a copy of 'The Little Orphan Waif's Crusade' straight away, alongside other gifts.

Click here to sign up for our mailing list, and receive your FREE stories.

CornerstoneTales.com/sign-up

LOVE VICTORIAN ROMANCE?

Other Rachel Downing Books

Two Steadfast Orphan's Dreams

Follow the stories of Isabella and Ada as they overcome all odds and find love.

Get 'Two Steadfast Orphan's Dreams' Here!

The Lost Orphans of Dark Streets

Follow the stories of Elizabeth and Molly as they negotiate the dangerous slums and find their place in the world.

Get 'The Lost Orphans of Dark Streets' Here!

The Orphan Prodigy's Stolen Tale

When ten-year-old Isabella Farmerson's world shatters with the tragic loss of her parents, she's thrust into a life of hardship and uncertainty.

Get 'The Orphan Prodigy's Stolen Tale' Here!

The Workhouse Orphan Rivals

Childhood sweethearts torn apart. A promise broken. A love that refuses to die.

Get 'The Workhouse Orphan Rivals' Here!

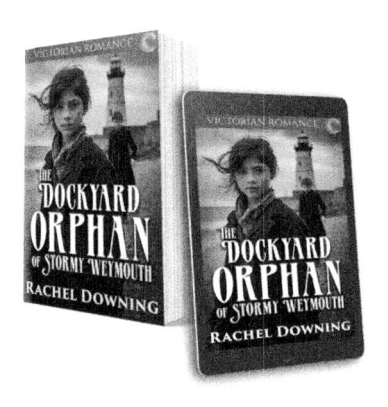

The Dockyard Orphan of Stormy Weymouth

Sarah Campbell's world crumbles when a tragic accident claims her parents' lives. She finds solace in the lighthouse's beam that guides ships to safety. But it's a young fisherman wrestling with his own loss, who truly captures her heart.

Get 'The Dockyard Orphan of Stormy Weymouth' Here!

And from our other Victorian Romance Author Dorothy Wellings...

The Moral Maid's Unjust Trial

Matilda must fend for herself when her father is wrongfully accused for a crime he didn't commit.

Get 'The Moral Maid's Unjust Trial' Here!

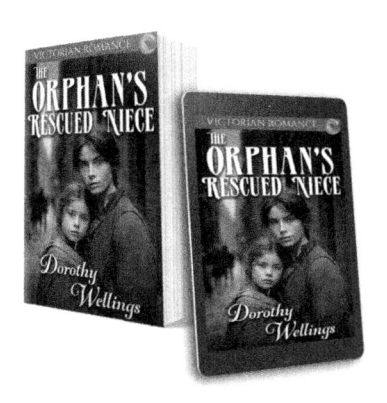

The Orphan's Rescued Niece

As Beatrice grows from a wide-eyed child into a resilient young woman, she finds herself caught between her love for her troubled brother and her desire for a life free from poverty and fear.

Get 'The Orphan's Rescued Niece' Here!

If you enjoyed this story, sign up to our mailing list to be the first to hear about our new releases and any sales and deals we have.

We also want to offer you a Victorian Romance novella - 'The Little Orphan Waif's Crusade' - absolutely free!

Click here to sign up for our mailing list, and receive your FREE stories.

CornerstoneTales.com/sign-up

Printed in Great Britain
by Amazon